GREAT SPORTS TEAMS

THE LOS ANGELES DODGERS

JOHN F. GRABOWSKI

Other Books in the Great Sports Teams Series:

GREAT SPORTS TEAMS

THE LOS ANGELES DODGERS

JOHN F. GRABOWSKI

LUCENT BOOKS®

THOMSON
™
GALE

San Diego • Detroit • New York • San Francisco • Cleveland
New Haven, Conn. • Waterville, Maine • London • Munich

For more information, contact
Lucent Books
10911 Technology Place,
San Diego, California 92127
Or you can visit our internet site at http://www.gale.com

Library of Congress Cataloging-in-Publication Data

Grabowski, John F.
    The Los Angeles Dodgers / by John F. Grabowski.
p. cm. — (Great sports teams)
Summary: Discusses the history, formation, and development of The Los
Angeles Dodgers baseball team, featuring players such as Sandy Koufax,
Don Drysdale, Maury Wills, Steve Garvey, Tommy Lasorda, and Fernando
Valenzuela.
Includes bibliographical references (p.) and index.
    ISBN 1-56006-941-4 (hardback. : alk. paper)
    1. Los Angeles Dodgers (Baseball team)—History—Juvenile literature.
2. Baseball players—United States—Biography—Juvenile literature [1. Los
Angeles Dodgers (Baseball team)—History. 2. Baseball—History. 3. Baseball
players.] I. Title: Los Angeles Dodgers. II. Title. III. Great sports teams
(Lucent Books)
    GV875.L6 G73 2003
    796.357′64′0979494—dc21

                                                          2002003262

Contents

FOREWORD

Former Supreme Court Chief Justice Warren Burger once said he always read the sports section of the newspaper first because it was about humanity's successes, while the front page listed only humanity's failures. Millions of people across the country today would probably agree with Burger's preference for tales of human endurance, record-breaking performances, and feats of athletic prowess. Although these accomplishments are far beyond what most Americans can ever hope to achieve, average people, the fans, do want to affect what happens on the field of play. Thus, their role becomes one of encouragement. They cheer for their favorite players and team and boo the opposition.

ABC Sports president Roone Arledge once attempted to explain the relationship between fan and team. Sport, said Arledge, is "a set of created circumstances—artificial circumstances—set up to frustrate a man in pursuit of a goal. He has to have certain skills to overcome those obstacles—or even to challenge them. And people who don't have those skills cheer him and admire him." Over a period of time, the admirers may develop a rabid—even irrational—allegiance to a particular team. Indeed, the word "fan" itself is derived from the word "fanatic," someone possessed by an excessive and irrational zeal. Sometimes this devotion to a team is because of a favorite player; often it's because of where a person lives, and, occasionally, it's because of a family allegiance to a particular club.

Whatever the reason, the bond formed between team and fan often defies reason. It may be easy to understand the appeal of the New York Yankees, a team that has gone to the World Series an incredible thirty-eight times and won twenty-six championships, nearly three times as many as any other major league baseball team. It is more difficult, though, to comprehend the fanaticism of Chicago Cubs fans, who faithfully follow the progress of a team that hasn't won a World Series since 1908. Regardless, the Cubs have surpassed the 2 million mark in home attendance in fourteen of the last seventeen years. In fact, their two highest totals were posted in 1999 and 2000, when the team finished in last place.

Each volume in Lucent's Great Sports Teams series examines a team that has left its mark on the "American sports consciousness." Each book looks at the history and tradition of the club in an attempt to understand its appeal and the loyalty—even passion—of its fans. Each volume also examines the lives and careers of people who played significant roles in the team's history. Players, managers, coaches, and front-office executives are represented.

Endnoted quotations help bring the text in each book to life. In addition, all books include an annotated bibliography and a For Further Reading list to supply students with sources for conducting additional individual research.

No one volume can hope to explain fully the mystique of the New York Yankees, Boston Celtics, Dallas Cowboys, or Montreal Canadiens. The Lucent Great Sports Teams series, however, gives interested readers a solid start on the road to understanding the mysterious bond that exists between modern professional sports teams and their devoted followers.

INTRODUCTION

The Transformation

When the Brooklyn Dodgers moved west to Los Angeles following the 1957 baseball season, few could have imagined how the team's image would be transformed by the relocation. In New York, the club was overshadowed by the mighty New York Yankees, who were baseball's royalty. To that point in time, the denizens of the Bronx had won twenty-three American League pennants and seventeen World Series titles, by far the most of any major-league club. Their all-time roster was dotted with names of baseball immortals such as Ruth, Gehrig, and DiMaggio. Rooting for such a team, noted comic Joe E. Lewis, was "like rooting for U.S. Steel [the largest steel producer in the United States and one of the largest industrial corporations in the world]."[1]

The Dodgers, on the other hand, were the favorites of the working class. Everyone who felt like an underdog could see themselves in the Dodgers, who were affectionately known as the Bums and whose roster had included players named Dazzy, Daffy, and Oisk. Brooklyn had won a respectable nine pennants since the modern era began in 1901, but just one championship. Even their National League archrivals, the New York Giants, had achieved more success. The team's fans were

The Brooklyn Dodgers in 1947. While in Brooklyn the Dodgers were never able to achieve the success of their local rivals, the New York Yankees.

used to heartbreak, annually moaning, "Wait till next year!" Though their followers were fanatical, attendance was limited by the cramped confines of tiny Ebbets Field, a ballpark built just prior to World War I.

All this changed, however, when the team moved to Los Angeles. In Los Angeles, the club had no competition from other teams in neighboring boroughs. All attention was focused on owner Walter O'Malley's new kids in town. With Los Angeles being the entertainment capital of the world, it wasn't long before television and movie stars became common sights at Dodger games. Attendance skyrocketed, with the club's fan base now consisting of a higher percentage of upper- and middle-class enthusiasts.

In 1962, by which time Los Angeles had already claimed a World Series for its own, the team took up residence in beautiful new Dodger Stadium located in Chavez Ravine. Drawing 2 and even 3 million fans in a season became a common occurrence. Management poured money back into the franchise, intent on providing the team's patrons with an attractive product. In an age of free agency, they succeeded in doing so to a surprising extent.

Perhaps no franchise has ever had its image reinvented to such a degree over such a relatively short period of time. The popularity and success of the Dodgers has made them one of the most attractive and valuable franchises in all of sports. In many ways, theirs is a story of the American dream come true.

CHAPTER 1

From Bums to Royalty

In some ways, the story of the Dodgers mirrors the story of the United States. Both the team and the nation began their existence in the eastern portion of the continent. After a period of time, each moved toward the West Coast in search of new opportunities. As the country has developed into the strongest, most powerful nation in the world, so, too, have the Dodgers become one of baseball's wealthiest, most successful teams.

Pre-Dodger Years

The forerunners of the modern-day Los Angeles Dodgers baseball team came into existence before the turn of the twentieth century. In 1884, businessman/attorney Charles Byrne and gamblers Joseph Doyle and Ferdinand "Gus" Abell pooled their money to form a baseball club known simply as the Brooklyns, or Brooklyners. The team, which was a member of the American Association (at that time a major league), played its home games in Washington Park in south Brooklyn near the site where George Washington's Continental army had fought the Battle of Long Island.

The Brooklyns finished ninth in the twelve-team league in their first season and followed up with three more losing years. In 1888, they hired Bill McGunnigle as their manager. McGunnigle helped turn the club around, and the team won its first pennant in 1889. Because a number of the club's players had married that spring and summer, the team became known as the Bridegrooms and finally, the Grooms.

The following season, Brooklyn switched from the American Association (which would fold after another year) to the older, more established National League. The team won another pennant its first year in the league, but a rift with the front office cost McGunnigle his job. John Montgomery Ward was hired to replace him, and the team moved its home games to Eastern Park for the 1891 season. "Ward's Wonders," as the team came to be called, dropped to sixth place that year, and despite a third-place finish the next season, Ward left the team to manage the New York Giants. His replacement was former Brooklyn player Dave Foutz.

The Brooklyn Bridegrooms in 1889, the year the team won its first pennant.

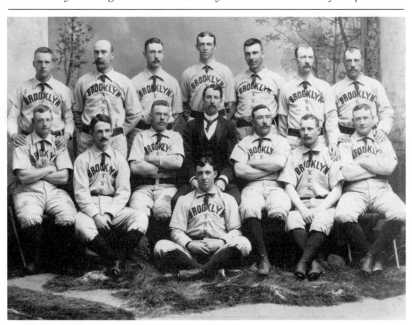

Foutz stayed at the club's helm for four years. "Foutz's Fillies" never finished higher than fifth, but along the way they picked up their current nickname. Because of the many trolley lines that ran near the ballpark, fans who came to the games were sometimes referred to as Trolley Dodgers. The name stuck with the team and was eventually shortened to Dodgers by the mid-1890s.

"The Squire of Brooklyn"

One of the team's early employees was a man named Charles Hercules Ebbets. Ebbets did everything from selling peanuts and scorecards to working as Byrne's assistant in the front office. Whenever he got the chance, he bought stock in the club. In 1897, he obtained a large block owned by Abell and gained a controlling interest in the team. The next year, "the Squire of Brooklyn" as Ebbets was referred to, bought some land in south Brooklyn and constructed a new playing facility called Washington Park.

The Dodgers finished tenth that season, and Ebbets was determined to change the team's fortunes. He reached an unusual agreement with Baltimore Orioles' owner Harry Von der Horst, giving Von der Horst 30 percent ownership in the Dodgers (which Ebbets would eventually buy back in 1900). As part of the deal, the Dodgers received several of Baltimore's best players, including future Hall of Famers Willie Keeler and Hughie Jennings. Orioles manager Ned Hanlon, another future Hall of Famer, took over the club, and the improvement was immediately apparent. Brooklyn won National League pennants in each of Hanlon's first two seasons. Since Hanlon's Superbas was the name of a successful vaudeville act of the day, the team began to be called the Superbas.

Hanlon's success was not long-lived. The American League, which began play as a major league in 1901, started raiding the older circuit for players, including several Brooklyn stars. Hanlon's club began to fall in the standings and by 1905 had dropped into last place, fifty-six and a half games out of first. The team would remain in the second division until 1915.

Uncle Robbie

By that time, Ebbets had constructed an imposing new $750,000 ballpark in Flatbush near the site of a garbage dump known as Pigtown. As he explained, "I've made more money than I ever expected to, but I am putting all of it, and more, too, into the new plant for the Brooklyn fans. . . . A club should provide a suitable home for its patrons."[2] The new stadium opened its doors for the first time on April 9, 1913.

The next year, Wilbert Robinson was hired and began an eighteen-year term as the team's manager. With him at the helm, the Superbas became known as the Robins and began to develop a heated rivalry with their Manhattan neighbors, the New York Giants. The Brooklyn clubs of this era featured many fine players, including Hall of Famer outfielder Zack Wheat, first baseman Jake Daubert (the first Brooklyn player ever to lead the league in batting), and future Yankees manager, Casey Stengel.

In 1916, Robinson led the team to its first pennant since 1900 and its first appearance ever in the World Series. There, the Robins lost to the Boston Red Sox and their young left-handed

The $750,000 Ebbets Field ballpark was built in 1913 for the Brooklyn Dodgers.

pitching sensation, Babe Ruth, in an exciting five-game set. The fans' joy was short-lived, however, as the club dropped back into the second division for the next three years.

In 1920, a revamped Brooklyn team, led by ace pitcher Burleigh Grimes, won the pennant once again. The Series that year was marked by several unusual events, including the first (and only) unassisted triple play in the history of the Fall Classic and the first grand slam in Series play.

Unfortunately, the Robins again came out on the losing side. This time, the Cleveland Indians defeated Brooklyn, five games to two. (This was the second of three seasons in which the Series was a best-of-nine-games affair.) Unbeknownst to Brooklyn fans, the team would not make it back to postseason play for more than two decades.

Most of Wilbert Robinson's term as manager was marked by mediocre, uninspired play. The team was firmly entrenched in the second division for most of the period, with only the play of the occasional stars such as Dazzy Vance, Dutch Reuther, and Babe Herman to keep the fans coming to the ballpark. Herman, an outstanding hitter and one of the most popular Dodgers ever (although called Robins at this time), entertained them with his escapades in the field and on the base paths. One of the most famous was when he doubled into a double play, ending up at third base along with two other teammates. Such misadventures helped endear him to the fans and helped contribute to the legend of what sports columnist John Lardner referred to as "Ebbets Field, the mother temple of daffiness in the national game."[3]

The Larry MacPhail Years

The team's fortunes took a turn for the better when Leland "Larry" MacPhail was hired as general manager in 1938. While serving in the same position with the Cincinnati Reds, he had brought many innovations to the game, including the introduction of night baseball. Now the man author Donald Honig referred to as a "hurricane . . . a man in motion, aggressive, dynamic, brimming with ideas"[4] would work his magic with the Dodgers. (With Robinson long gone, the team returned to—and officially adopted—the name Dodgers.)

To generate interest among the fans, one of MacPhail's first moves was to hire the immortal Babe Ruth as a coach. The team still finished in seventh place his first year, but made money for the first time since 1920. The next season, MacPhail hired fiery Leo Durocher as manager. In ensuing years, he acquired players such as Dolph Camilli, Joe Medwick, Kirby Higbe, Dixie Walker, Pee Wee Reese, and Pete Reiser to help transform the team into a perennial pennant contender. The club that had won only two pennants in the thirty-seven years prior to MacPhail would win seven in the nineteen years after his arrival. It just missed another in 1946 when it tied St. Louis for first place, then lost to the Cardinals in the first-ever play-off series.

Jackie Robinson and the Boys of Summer

Although the team was now officially called the Dodgers, it picked up other unofficial nicknames along the way. Among them were the Daffiness Boys (by sportswriter Westbrook Pegler) and the Bums (immortalized by sports cartoonist Willard Mullin). One of the most romantic of these names was the Boys of Summer, affixed to the team by author Roger Kahn (who borrowed the phrase from a Dylan Thomas poem). The Boys of Summer refers to the Brooklyn teams of the late 1940s and early 1950s, when the club was a National League power-house. They won their first pennant in 1941, losing to the New York Yankees in the World Series. (The two clubs would meet in the Fall Classic six more times over the next fifteen years.)

The 1940s also saw an event of historic importance occur on the baseball scene. In 1946, Branch Rickey (who had replaced MacPhail as the Dodgers' general manager when the latter went to join the war effort) signed Jackie Robinson to a profes-sional contract. The next year, Robinson became the first black player in the major leagues since Welday and Fleet Walker in 1884. He helped the Dodgers to win the pennant, garnering Rookie of the Year honors along the way.

With Robinson having broken the color line, the Dodgers became one of the most aggressive teams in signing black players. Roy Campanella, Don Newcombe, Joe Black, and Junior Gilliam all played important roles in the club's success. Together with

Jackie Robinson, Duke Snider, Roy Campanella, and Gil Hodges (left to right) pose in 1953. These outstanding players contributed largely to the Dodgers' success in the late 1940s and early 1950s.

Duke Snider, Gil Hodges, Carl Furillo, Carl Erskine, and Billy Cox, they formed the nucleus of a team that would win three more pennants from 1948 to 1954. (They narrowly missed another pennant when they were victimized by Bobby Thomson's "Shot Heard 'Round the World" in the 1951 play-off against the Giants. The three-run home run in the bottom half of the ninth inning of the final game gave the Giants the pennant.) Unfortunately, the Yankees defeated them in the World Series each time, ending their drive for a title.

The Ecstasy . . .

Brooklyn's long wait for a championship, however, would soon be over. Walter Alston took over as manager in 1954 and guided the team to a second-place finish behind their archrivals, the Giants. The next year, the Dodgers broke quickly from the gate, winning twenty-two of their first twenty-four games.

They never broke stride and won the pennant by thirteen and a half games (their largest margin of victory ever).

Their opponents in the World Series, once again, were the hated Yankees. This time, however, Brooklyn came out on top, defeating the New Yorkers in seven games. Among the team's heroes was twenty-two-year-old left-hander Johnny Podres, who won two games. His 2–0 shutout in Game 7 gave the Dodgers their first world championship in their eighth try.

The Dodgers won the pennant again in 1956, this time edging out the Milwaukee Braves by one game and the Cincinnati Reds by two. They could not repeat their success in the Series, as the Yankees bounced back to beat them in another seven-game affair. The Series was highlighted by the Yankees' Don Larsen's perfect game in Game 5. The pain felt by Brooklyn fans, however, was nothing compared with what was to come in 1957.

. . . And the Agony

In 1944, a group of investors that included attorney Walter F. O'Malley had bought a large block of stock in the Dodgers' organization. The next year, the group purchased a controlling interest. President and general manager Branch Rickey eventually sold his share of the club to O'Malley, who took over as president in 1950.

By the mid-1950s, O'Malley had begun looking for a new home for the team to replace the antiquated and relatively tiny Ebbets Field. When his attempt to buy a site for a larger stadium was turned down by the city, he looked west to California. Despite a strong public outcry, O'Malley eventually announced plans to move the team to Los Angeles, envisioning tremendous profits in a region with no major-league team of its own. The fans of Brooklyn were devastated. As author Dan Okrent said, "It ripped at the loyalties of people who felt that the teams were as loyal to them as they were to the teams. . . . It was probably the first time in . . . thirty years that fans were reminded that this was a business as much as it was a game."[5]

In addition to a new home, O'Malley's grand plan included some nearby competition. He convinced owner Horace Stoneham of the financially strapped Giants to move west with him.

Stoneham agreed to relocate his club to San Francisco. After the final game of the 1957 season, nearly sixty years of National League baseball in New York City came to an end.

The Start of a New Era

The image of the Bums was left behind as West Coast fans greeted the team with open arms. Many of the Boys of Summer made the trip west with the team, but expectations for the future lay with young hopefuls such as Sandy Koufax, Don Drysdale, Ron Fairly, Frank Howard, and John Roseboro.

The Dodgers played their last game in Ebbets Field on September 24, 1957. Less than seven months later, on April 18, 1958, they played their first regular season home game in the ninety-two-thousand-seat Los Angeles Coliseum, which would be their home for their first four years on the West Coast. The players paraded through downtown Los Angeles on the morning of the game, then proceeded to the Coliseum. There, before a National League–record crowd of 78,672, they defeated the Giants by a score of 6–5.

Despite its large seating capacity, the Coliseum was less than ideal for baseball. The stadium's configuration forced the field to be laid out in such a way that the left field fence was only 251 feet from home plate. Deep center field, on the other hand, was 440 feet away. Even a screen erected to eliminate cheap home runs to left was not successful. "Chinese homers" was the term coined to describe pop-ups hit over the fence.

On the field, the 1958 season was hardly a success for the Dodgers. They finished in seventh place, just two games out of the cellar. At the gate, however, they exceeded expectations, with fans coming in droves to see the new team in town. They surpassed their attendance for their last season in Ebbets Field by the All-Star break, and finished the year having drawn 1,845,556 fans to the Coliseum, the highest total in the franchise's long history.

The next year, the Dodgers rewarded their fans with one of the greatest turnarounds in big-league history. Bolstered by the arrival of rookies Maury Wills and Frank Howard and the emergence of pitchers Sandy Koufax and Don Drysdale, the team finished the year in a tie for first place with the Milwaukee

Braves. They proceeded to defeat Milwaukee in a best-of-three play-off to give California its first pennant ever, and the team's fifth of the decade. It was the first time in National League history that a team had gone from seventh place to first in consecutive seasons.

The Dodgers' opponents in the 1959 World Series were the Chicago White Sox, who had not played in the Fall Classic since 1919. The clubs played before a total of 420,784 fans in the six-game matchup, a Series record up to that time. An amazing 92,394 showed up at the Coliseum for Game 3. That new mark lasted just one day, however, as 92,650 more came out for Game 4.

After being shut out in the opener, Los Angeles bounced back to take the next three games. Pitcher Sandy Koufax lost a 1–0 decision in Game 5, but the team came back to take Game 6 by a score of 9–3. The Dodgers were champions of the world in only their second year in Los Angeles.

The first pitch of the 1959 World Series. The Dodgers defeated the Chicago White Sox in six games for the championship.

As quickly as the Dodgers had risen in 1959, so did they fall in 1960. Age began to take its toll on many of the players, and the team fell to fourth place in the National League standings, thirteen games behind the pennant-winning Pittsburgh Pirates. Despite the team's disappointing showing, fans continued to pour through the turnstiles. The club set another franchise attendance record by drawing 2,253,887 to its games. (The team had surpassed the 2 million mark in attendance for the first time in 1959.)

The Taj O'Malley

The Dodgers rebounded in 1961 and remained in the pennant race until late in the season. They finished in second and ended their tenancy in the Coliseum. The 1962 season found them in their new home, a beautiful new ballpark in Chavez Ravine known as Dodger Stadium. It was the dream palace Walter O'Malley had envisioned ever since announcing his move west.

O'Malley's magnificent new $18 million edifice was designed by New York architect Emil Praeger. It was quickly dubbed the Taj O'Malley by local sportswriters and is still considered by many to be the most beautiful major-league park. The clean, multidecked grandstand is covered by distinctive zigzag roofs. The stadium, with its breathtaking views of downtown Los Angeles and the San Gabriel Mountains, formally opened on April 10, 1962, before 52,564 fans.

The team seemed to be inspired by its new surroundings. It was in first place for much of the year before finally finishing in a tie with the San Francisco Giants. The teams played a three-game play-off for the right to go to the World Series, and, just like in 1951, the Dodgers came out on the short end.

Despite the depressing finish, the Dodgers' 1962 season was marked by many great individual performances. Sandy Koufax hurled a no-hitter and tied a record by striking out eighteen batters in a single game. Maury Wills set a record by stealing an incredible 104 bases. Don Drysdale won twenty-five games, and Tommy Davis won the batting title with a mark of .346. He also drove in 153 runs, a Los Angeles record that has not been matched. Off the field, Jackie Robinson became the first black elected to the Baseball Hall of Fame.

*An aerial view of the spectacular Dodger Stadium on opening day,
April 10, 1962.*

Pitching and Speed

Aside from slugger Frank Howard, the Dodger teams of this period did not have many home run threats. They did, however,
have great pitching and great speed. From 1963 to 1966, that
was enough to lead them to three pennants and a pair of World
Series titles—in 1963 over the New York Yankees and in 1965
against the Minnesota Twins.

Unfortunately, 1966 marked the great Koufax's final
season—he was forced to retire from the game at age thirty-
one. Some of the slack was picked up by Claude Osteen, who
was obtained in a trade with Washington, and Don Sutton,
who was brought up from the minors in 1966 and would go on

to win over three hundred games in his career. When the club plummeted to eighth place after winning the pennant that year, it was obvious changes would have to be made.

Luckily, the Dodgers' farm system was one of the most productive in all of baseball. Youngsters such as Ted Sizemore, Steve Garvey, Bill Buckner, and Bill Russell were groomed to take their place on the team, replacing older, less productive players. The "Mod Squad" of these years had the team back on the rise by 1969 when the league was reorganized into two six-team divisions.

By this point, Peter O'Malley had replaced his father as president of the team (the youngest president in the majors). Walter had stepped up to become chairman of the board. Al Campanis, formerly the head of the scouting department, took over the duties of general manager.

On the field, the team remained competitive. It finally returned to the top, taking its first Western Division title in 1974. The "Babes of Summer," as sportswriter Frank Finch dubbed them, won 102 games during the regular season. They made it all the way to the World Series led by Andy Messersmith, Cy Young Award winner Mike Marshall, and the infield of Garvey, Davey Lopes, Ron Cey, and Bill Russell (a quartet that would play together for a major-league record nine seasons). The Dodgers lost to Charlie Finley's Oakland Athletics in the Series, but the future looked bright for the young team.

Continuing a Winning Tradition

Walter Alston finished his twenty-three-year career as the Dodgers' manager with second place finishes in both 1975 and 1976. He retired and was replaced at the helm by former Dodgers' pitcher Tommy Lasorda. The outgoing Lasorda was of a completely different temperament than his predecessor. While Alston was the strong, silent type, Lasorda bounced around in the dugout, hugging players after big hits and encouraging them with a constant stream of chatter.

As a coach under Alston and former manager in the Dodgers' farm system, Lasorda was already familiar with most of the team's players. They responded to his cheerleading by winning pennants in each of his first two seasons (making him only the second National League manager to accomplish the feat). The fans responded by coming out in record numbers, with the team surpassing the 3 million mark in attendance for the first time in 1978. Unfortunately, the Dodgers were defeated by the Yankees in the World Series both years.

After a two-year hiatus, the Dodgers won the pennant again in 1981 with the help of rookie pitching sensation Fernando Valenzuela. In the Series that year, they gained a measure of revenge by defeating the Yankees to give them their fourth championship since moving west.

With Lasorda at the helm, the Dodgers won three more division crowns in the decade, the most memorable coming in 1988. That year, a club many observers predicted would finish as low as fourth won the division by seven games. Led by Cy Young Award winner Orel Hershiser, the Dodgers proceeded to upset the New York Mets in an exciting National League Championship Series. Kirk Gibson's dramatic pinch-hit home run in the bottom of the ninth inning gave Los Angeles a win in Game 1 of the World Series, and the Dodgers went on to defeat the Oakland Athletics for the world championship.

The Second Hundred Years

The 1990 season marked the Dodgers' one hundredth anniversary as a member of the National League. The new decade saw several bright new faces burst onto the Los Angeles baseball scene. Eric Karros, Mike Piazza, Raul Mondesi, Hideo Nomo, and Todd Hollandsworth each won Rookie of the Year honors—amazingly, in successive seasons. With the help of the new blood, the team made two appearances in postseason play (1995, 1996) but could not advance past the division series either year.

In 1996, Lasorda stepped down as manager after suffering a mild heart attack. He was replaced by former shortstop Bill Russell. A year later, Lasorda was given the sport's highest honor when he was elected to the Baseball Hall of Fame.

Despite not winning a pennant in the decade (the first time since the 1930s), the Dodgers still finished with the best overall record among Western Division teams in the 1990s. As the new

Manager Tommy Lasorda and pitcher Orel Hershiser hold up the 1988 World Championship trophy.

millennium began, promising young players such as Adrian Beltre and Shawn Green gave the team hope for continuing its winning tradition.

Whether in good times or in bad, Los Angeles fans have always come out in support of their team. Since moving west in 1958, the Dodgers have never played before less than 1 million fans at home. They have surpassed the 2 million mark in attendance in each of the last twenty-nine seasons, and broken the 3 million plateau fifteen times since 1980. They are one of the most valuable franchises in sports today.

CHAPTER 2

Sandy Koufax

During the five-year period from 1962 to 1966, Sandy Koufax was one of the most dominating pitchers major-league baseball has ever seen. He had the best earned run average in the National League in each of those seasons, won four strikeout crowns and three Cy Young Awards, and compiled a cumulative record of 111 wins against only 34 losses. His blazing fastball and knee-buckling curve were the bane of hitters around the league.

Unfortunately, Koufax was hindered by a painful form of arthritis. His physical problems caused him to retire at the age of thirty-one, at the height of his career. What records and standards he might have set can only be left to the imagination.

The Boy from Brooklyn

Sanford Braun was born in the Borough Park section of Brooklyn, New York, on December 30, 1935. His parents, Jack and Evelyn, were divorced when Sandy was just three years old. Six years later, Evelyn married a prominent New York lawyer named Irving Koufax, who raised the boy as his own.

As a youngster, Sandy played the street sports common to all Brooklyn boys. Stoopball, stickball, and punchball were all popular activities in the school yards, playgrounds, and parks of the borough. When his mother remarried, the family briefly relocated to Rockville Centre in Long Island. The move almost had tragic consequences for Sandy. One day, while he was riding his bike, he was hit by a car. He hurt his knee, but luckily, the injury was not severe. He quickly recuperated and was able to take part in the sports he so loved.

The Koufax family eventually returned to Brooklyn, where Sandy enrolled in Lafayette High School in 1949. While there, he discovered a new love: basketball. He averaged 16.5 points per game while serving as team captain as a senior and seemed to have a future in the sport. He continued to sharpen his skills outside of school by playing in a Jewish Community House (JCH) league.

Sandy also tried out for the Lafayette baseball team

A portrait of pitcher Sandy Koufax in 1955, his first year as a Brooklyn Dodger.

and made it as a first baseman. (One of the pitchers on the squad was Freddie Wilpon, who would later become part owner of the New York Mets.) Koufax's strong left arm attracted the attention of Milt Laurie, the father of two of Sandy's teammates and manager of the Parkviews, a local sandlot team. Laurie, himself a former semipro player, convinced Koufax he had the talent to be a successful pitcher. "You've got a big-league arm," he told Sandy. "I'd like to work with you."[6] Sandy agreed to work with Laurie.

Sandy discovered that he liked pitching. He enjoyed being in control of the game, and delighted in being able to throw his fastball past opposing hitters. He experienced some early success, hurling a no-hitter in one of his first games for the Parkviews.

Koufax's talent, however, had to be developed. He had an exceptionally strong arm but lacked control. He attracted the interest of a few big-league scouts, but when he was offered a basketball scholarship to the University of Cincinnati, he put baseball on hold. As he later said, "The last thing that entered my mind was becoming a professional athlete."[7]

Koufax was the third-leading scorer on the freshman basketball team at Cincinnati under coach Ed Jucker. Jucker was also coach of the varsity baseball team. Sandy made the squad as a pitcher and went 3–1, with an impressive fifty-one strikeouts in thirty-one innings in his one college season. More scouts began to come around, and on December 14, 1954, two weeks before his nineteenth birthday, Sandy signed with the Dodgers. His contract called for a bonus of fourteen thousand dollars and an annual salary of six thousand dollars for both 1955 and 1956. Amazingly, it was given to a youngster who had pitched fewer than twenty games in his life. Despite his inexperience, his strong left arm and ability to throw a ball more than ninety miles an hour was enough to make Brooklyn think he was worth the money.

The rule at the time stated that if a player was paid a bonus of more than four thousand dollars, he had to be kept on the big-league roster for two full years. The only players paid such bonuses were the best prospects who teams felt would become stars after gaining experience. Unfortunately, it usually worked out that these players languished on the bench for two years,

*Eighteen-year-old Koufax smiles for reporters after signing a lucrative
contract with the Dodgers in 1954.*

gaining little experience because of their lack of playing time.
With their development hindered, they rarely reached the levels
expected of them.

Bonus Baby

Koufax reported to Vero Beach, Florida, for his first spring
training in March 1955. He joined a veteran team, with many of
its stars in the prime years of their careers. It was no wonder
that the inexperienced teenager's performance left something
to be desired. "I was so nervous and tense," said Koufax, "I
couldn't throw the ball for ten days. When I finally started
pitching, I felt I should throw as hard as I could. I wound up
with an arm so sore that I had to rest for another week."[8]

After the Dodgers completed training camp, they began the
season by winning twenty-two of their first twenty-four
games. Before he was able to make a contribution to the team,
however, Sandy was injured. He stepped on a sprinkler head
while shagging fly balls in practice one day and suffered a hair-
line fracture in his ankle. He was placed on the thirty-day disabled list, where he remained until June 8.

Koufax did not play in a game until late June when he hurled two innings of relief against the Milwaukee Braves. Two weeks later, he made his first start against the Pittsburgh Pirates. He walked eight batters and struck out four in less than five innings but did not get a decision. He gave a hint as to his potential when he picked up his first victory on August 27. Pitching against the Cincinnati Reds, Koufax threw a two-hit shutout, striking out fourteen batters in the process. It was the most batters struck out in a single game by a National League pitcher all year.

Koufax shows his pleasure at seeing his name on the team roster in 1956. The pitcher's first two seasons with the Dodgers were lackluster.

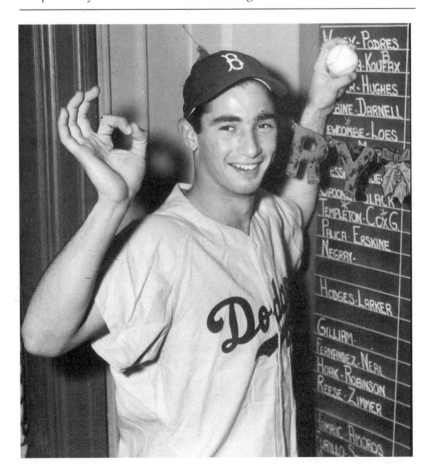

In Koufax's next appearance, however, the Braves pummeled him in a one-inning outing in relief. He followed that up with another shutout in his next start against the Pittsburgh Pirates. Koufax finished the season with two wins and two losses in twelve appearances. He had demonstrated the ability to throw the ball with great velocity but, like many young pitchers, had been inconsistent with his control. The Dodgers had used their fast start to breeze to the National League pennant. They then defeated the Yankees in the World Series for their first-ever championship. Although Koufax did not see any action in the Series, he received a check for $9,768.21 as his share for being a member of the winning club.

The 1956 season was more of the same for Koufax. He played in sixteen games and pitched less than fifty-nine innings. He had a record of 2–4 to show for his brief action, with an earned run average of just under five runs per game. "He really should have been in A ball [the minor leagues]," said former pitching teammate Ed Roebuck, "learning how to throw strikes. But Sandy never pitched a day in the minors."[9]

A New Start in a New City

Because Koufax had spent a month on the disabled list in 1955, his two years on the major-league roster would not be up until thirty days into the 1957 season. In effect, he had one month to prove to manager Walter Alston that he should not be sent down to the minors to gain more experience. As luck would have it, on May 16, just before the thirty-day period was about to expire, Koufax pitched against the Chicago Cubs. He had an outstanding game, hurling a four-hit, complete game 3–2 victory. Although he walked seven batters in the contest, he also struck out fourteen. Manager Alston was so impressed he decided to keep him on the roster.

Koufax had several other moments of glory that season, hurling three more games in which he reached double figures in strikeouts. For the most part, however, his pitching remained inconsistent. The Dodgers struggled for most of the year, and before the season was over, owner Walter O'Malley announced that the team would be moving to Los Angeles for the 1958 season (a move particularly upsetting to the Brooklyn-born

Koufax). In the final game of the year, the Dodgers trailed the Philadelphia Phillies by a score of 2–1. Koufax came in to relieve the starting pitcher in the bottom half of the eighth inning, and when the Dodgers failed to score in the ninth, he became the last man to throw a pitch for the Brooklyn Dodgers.

Glimpses of Greatness

With the move to Los Angeles, Koufax finally got his chance to be a regular starting pitcher after several impressive early-season outings. By the beginning of July, he had pitched well enough to compile a record of 7–3. In his next start, however, he injured his ankle on a play at first base. He struggled after returning from the injury and finished the season with eleven wins and eleven losses. Considering that the team finished twenty-one games under .500, he had not pitched badly. At the same time, however, he knew he was capable of a better performance.

Over the next two years, Koufax teased the Dodgers and their fans with glimpses of his potential. In the world championship season of 1959, his record was just 8–6. Included among his victories, however, was a complete game win over the Phillies in which he struck out sixteen batters to set a new major-league record for a night game. The record would last just over two months.

On August 31, Koufax fanned eighteen San Francisco Giants in another evening contest to set a new record. Koufax had struck out thirteen Phillies in his previous start, giving him a record-tying thirty-one in the two consecutive outings. In his next start, he fanned ten in a loss to the Cubs. The forty-one strikeouts over a three-game span set yet another major-league mark.

In the World Series against the Chicago White Sox that fall, Koufax hurled two scoreless innings in relief in Game 1. He followed up with a sterling performance as the Game 5 starter before more than ninety-two thousand fans in the Coliseum. He held the Sox to just one run over seven innings, but the Dodgers failed to score and he lost the game. When Los Angeles bounced back to take the Series by winning Game 6 by a score of 9–3, Koufax earned his second championship ring in five big-league seasons.

Koufax could throw a devastating fastball, but he struggled with control during his first few years with the Dodgers.

Despite signs that Koufax was beginning to fulfill his potential in 1959, the 1960 season was a disappointing one for Koufax and the Dodgers. The club dropped to fourth place as Koufax struggled along to an 8–13 record. Included among his games were a one-hit shutout over Pittsburgh and two fifteen-strikeout games.

Control continued to bedevil him, however. Koufax's answer to any difficult situation he faced on the mound was to try to throw the ball harder. The result was usually the opposite of what he hoped for. By this point, after six big-league seasons, Koufax's lifetime record was 36–40. He began to have serious doubts about ever becoming a star in the major leagues. Said Kevin Kennedy, former Texas Rangers manager and a close friend of Koufax, "He was seriously thinking about leaving baseball."[10]

The Turning Point

By the time Koufax arrived for spring training in 1961, he had reached a decision: He would give himself one more year in which to succeed or else seriously consider another profession. He didn't realize it at the time, but the event that would change the course of his career was near at hand.

The Dodgers' second-string players were flying to Orlando one day to play an exhibition game against the Minnesota Twins. Sitting next to Koufax on the plane was his roommate, catcher Norm Sherry. Sherry had often mentioned that he thought Koufax tried to throw the ball too hard. He repeated a suggestion he had made many times in the past. "All this is is a B game," he said. "If you get behind the hitters, don't try to throw hard because when you force your fast ball you're always high with it. Just this once, try it my way like we've talked about. If you get into trouble, let up and throw the curve and try to pitch to spots."[11]

For whatever reason, this time Koufax agreed. He proceeded to hurl seven no-hit innings against the Twins, striking out eight batters and walking five. Sherry's message had finally sunk in. By not trying to overpower the hitters, Koufax was better able to control where the ball was going. The missing piece of the puzzle was now in place.

When the season started, Koufax proved he had learned his lesson well. After losing his first game, he won nine of his next ten starts to earn his first selection to the National League All-Star team. His performance dropped off somewhat in the second half of the year, but he still finished with a career-high eighteen victories. He also set a single-season league record for strikeouts, fanning 269 batters.

Just as Koufax had been the last Dodger to throw a pitch in Brooklyn, he was also the last to pitch in the Los Angeles Coliseum. He hurled a thirteen-inning complete game victory over the Chicago Cubs that day, striking out fifteen batters in the process. Koufax used his blazing fastball and sharp-breaking curveball to perfection. He had made the transition that escapes so many young pitchers. He had learned how to pitch rather than just how to throw.

The Best of the Best

Over the next five years, Koufax pitched as well as any player had before or since. His highlights for 1962 included an eighteen-strikeout game (to tie his major-league mark) and a no-hitter against the expansion New York Mets. Circulatory problems in the index finger of his pitching hand forced him to miss time, and he finished the year with a record of 14–7. He led the league in earned run average, however, with a mark of 2.54.

Koufax really blossomed in 1963. He won twenty-five games, struck out a record 306 batters, hurled eleven shutouts,

---

Koufax beams as manager Walter Alston points to a message board proclaiming the pitcher's no-hitter against the New York Mets in 1962.

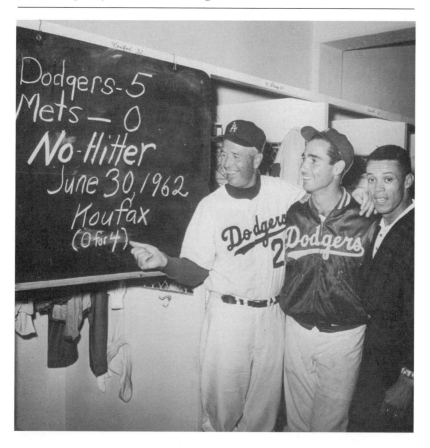

and tossed the second no-hitter of his career. For his heroics, he won both the Most Valuable Player (MVP) Award, and Cy Young Award as the game's best pitcher. As first baseman Ron Fairly described Koufax's dominance, "There were actually times that year when I felt sorry for the other team's hitter. I would think, 'He's not even gonna foul tip one.' And then he wouldn't."[12]

Koufax continued his masterful pitching in the World Series against the Yankees. In Game 1, he set a new Series record by striking out fifteen New Yorkers in a magnificent six-hit 5–2 win. His dominance was perhaps best summarized by Yankee catcher Yogi Berra. "I can see how he won twenty-five games," said the future Hall of Famer. "What I don't understand is how he lost five."[13]

Koufax followed up with a 2–1 victory in Game 4, giving the Dodgers a four-game sweep and the world championship. He added the World Series MVP Award to his trophy case, then followed up by winning the Hickock Belt as the Professional Athlete of the Year.

A problem with his pitching mechanics caused Koufax to struggle out of the gate in 1964. He was finishing the pitching motion off balance because of throwing across his body. He was just 4–4 before pitching coach Joe Becker helped him correct the flaw. He then proceeded to win eleven games in a row, including the third no-hitter of his career. An elbow injury in August, however, cut his season short. Doctors diagnosed his problem as a form of arthritis that could be controlled, but not cured. He finished the year with a 19–5 record and his fourth consecutive earned run average title. The problem with his health, however, could not be ignored. He spent the winter worrying about his uncertain future.

A Magical Season

The next spring, Koufax's elbow continued to swell up, but cortisone shots helped keep the swelling under control. He got into a routine of putting ice on his elbow after pitching, and the results were nothing short of miraculous. His pitching was as good as ever as he led the National League in nearly every major pitching category. His marks for wins (26),

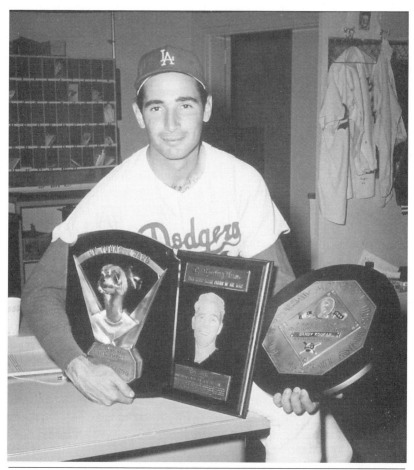

Koufax displays some of the award plaques he received during his breakout 1963 season, including the coveted Cy Young and Most Valuable Player awards.

winning percentage (.765), earned run average (2.04), complete games (27), innings pitched (335.2), and strikeouts (a record 382) all topped the circuit. In addition, he started and won the annual All-Star Game in July.

On September 9, Koufax made history by hurling a perfect game against the Chicago Cubs. He became the first major-league pitcher to hurl four no-hitters, doing so, incredibly, in four consecutive seasons.

As amazing as Koufax's accomplishments were during the regular season, he surpassed himself in the World Series against the Minnesota Twins. The Series opened on Yom Kippur, the holiest of Jewish holidays. Sticking to his religious convictions, Koufax did not pitch that day. He came back to pitch Game 2, but lost by a score of 5–1. With the Series tied at two games apiece, Koufax took the ball for Game 5 and hurled a brilliant 7–0 shutout. When the Twins won Game 6 back in Minnesota, the Series went to the seventh game.

Koufax took the mound for Game 7, pitching on just two days' rest. Incredibly, he limited the hard-hitting Twins to just three hits and threw another shutout to give the Dodgers the championship. Koufax was named the Most Valuable Player of the Series for the second time in his career. He followed that up with his second Cy Young Award. He finished the year with a second Hickock Belt as 1965's Professional Athlete of the Year.

The Holdouts

After his magnificent 1965 season, Koufax was not happy with the $80,000 contract offered by the Dodgers for 1966. In an unprecedented move, he teamed up with fellow pitcher Don Drysdale and held out for more money. The two stars requested $1 million over three years, to be divided evenly between the two of them. The Dodgers responded by offering Koufax $100,000 and Drysdale $85,000.

The two pitchers stuck to their beliefs and prepared to sit out the year. Finally, just before the season was scheduled to open, the players and team reached an agreement. Koufax signed for $125,000 and Drysdale for $110,000, making them the highest-paid players in the major leagues. The team still got a bargain. In today's terms, the contracts would be worth less than $1 million each—far below the going rate for top players.

With his contract negotiations behind him, Koufax began the season after having missed most of spring training. It didn't seem to affect him in the least. Koufax produced career highs in both wins (27) and earned run average (1.73). He led the league in the latter category for the fifth straight time. He also surpassed the three hundred–strikeout mark for the third time in his career.

Koufax topped his year with a pennant-clinching win over the Philadelphia Phillies on the last day of the regular season. After a hard pennant race, however, the Dodgers were no match for the Baltimore Orioles in the World Series. Baltimore swept four straight games to take the title. Koufax lost Game 2 despite giving up just one run in six innings. Although no one realized it at the time, it would be his last appearance on a major-league mound.

A Career Cut Short

On November 18, Koufax shocked the sports world by announcing his retirement from baseball at the age of thirty-one. He cited continued problems with his arthritic elbow as the reason for his early departure. "I was getting cortisone shots with pretty good regularity," he said. "And I just feel like I don't want to take a chance on completely disabling myself."[14] Some skeptics suggested it might be a bargaining ploy to get a

Fans deluge Koufax with requests for autographs in 1967, the year he announced his retirement from baseball at the young age of thirty-one.

better contract, but Koufax turned down an offer of $150,000 from the Dodgers for 1967.

After leaving the game as an active player, Koufax was a commentator for NBC sports from 1967 to 1972. He also dealt in real estate and raised show horses. In 1979, Koufax returned to the Dodgers to take the position of roving minor-league pitching instructor. In more recent times, he has visited spring training camps in Florida and given informal instruction to young pitchers.

On July 19, 1972, Koufax was awarded baseball's highest honor, being voted into the Hall of Fame in Cooperstown, New York. At age thirty-six, he was the youngest man so honored. It was the crowning achievement for a pitcher who led the National League in earned run average five times, strikeouts four times, wins three times, and winning percentage, complete games, and innings pitched twice in his career. Although a few other pitchers have compiled comparable statistics, none ever did so over a shorter period of time. It is no wonder that many consider him the greatest left-handed pitcher of all time.

CHAPTER 3

Don Drysdale

Few major-league pitchers have been as intimidating as six-foot six-inch-tall Don Drysdale. As former San Francisco Giant first baseman Orlando Cepeda put it, "The trick against Drysdale is to hit him before he hits you."[15] When the intimidation factor was combined with a great arm and excellent control, the result was one of baseball's all-time great power pitchers. Drysdale won more than two hundred games in his career and struck out more than two hundred batters six times. He was enshrined in the Baseball Hall of Fame twelve years after pitching partner Sandy Koufax.

The Road to Brooklyn

Donald Scott Drysdale was born in the sunny town of Van Nuys, California, on July 23, 1936. His father—Scott Sumner Drysdale—worked at the Pacific Telephone and Telegraph Company. Scott had been a minor-league pitcher with the Los Angeles Angels of the Pacific Coast League but had to give up his dream of a big-league career when he developed back problems. Scott married Verna Ruth Ley, and the couple had two children: Don and a younger daughter, Nancy.

As a child in Southern California, Don participated in all sports but did not harbor dreams of becoming a ballplayer. He played on his first organized baseball team at age nine in the Valley Junior Baseball League. At Van Nuys High School, the six-foot two-inch youngster was a backup quarterback on the football team and an infielder on the baseball squad. Don did not begin pitching until he was sixteen years old. One day, the starting pitcher on his American Legion (a nationwide youth baseball program) team failed to show up for a game. Don's dad, who coached the team, picked him to pitch in his place. For advice, he simply said, "Don't get cute and throw strikes."[16]

Don hurled a complete game victory and impressed Brooklyn Dodgers' scout Gordie Holt, who happened to be in the stands. Holt invited him to play with the Brooklyn Dodger Juniors, a team run by Holt and another Dodger scout, Lefty Phillips. Unfortunately, a leg injury sidelined Don for all but a handful of games.

By the time Don entered his last year at Van Nuys High School in the fall of 1953, he had grown four inches and developed a real interest in pitching. As a senior, he won ten of his eleven games, tossed a no-hitter, and made the All-City team. His strong right arm attracted the attention of several more scouts. He was offered a contract by the Pittsburgh Pirates but instead signed with the Dodgers, in part out of loyalty to Gordie Holt. Drysdale's contract called for a $2,200 bonus and a salary of $600 a month.

Education of a Pitcher

Drysdale began his pro career with the Dodgers' Bakersfield farm team of the Class C California League. He compiled an 8–5 record, then moved to Montreal of the Triple-A International League in 1955. There, he was 10–2 by midseason when he broke a bone in his hand. He tried to hide the injury, but lost nine of his last ten games.

Drysdale's hand healed by the time spring training came around in 1956. The Dodgers had won the World Series the previous fall, but a series of injuries had created openings on their pitching staff. Drysdale had a good spring and was told by Dodgers' general manager Buzzie Bavasi that he had made

Intimidating and powerful, six-foot six-inch Don Drysdale was one of the greatest Dodgers pitchers of all time.

the big-league team. He was also given some words of advice. "There's always going to be somebody else wanting to take your job," said Bavasi. "There will always be some new kids in the wings. So, don't ever take anything for granted."[17] Drysdale never forgot those words.

Drysdale made his major-league debut with two innings of relief work against the Philadelphia Phillies on opening day. His first big-league victory came a few weeks later on April 24 against those same Phillies. The twenty-year-old Drysdale went 5–5 as a rookie, with four of his wins coming against the Dodgers' hated crosstown rivals, the New York Giants. That was enough to make him an immediate hit with Brooklyn fans.

Nineteen-year-old Drysdale and Walter Alston share a victory smile after the rookie pitcher won his first major-league game against the Phillies.

A player who had a big influence on Drysdale was veteran pitcher Sal "the Barber" Maglie, who the Dodgers had acquired from the Giants. Maglie's nickname came from the way he "shaved" opposing batters with his close pitches. His aggressive style of pitching made an impression on the young Drysdale. As he later explained, "I decided I wasn't going to let any batter get in the way of my winning a ballgame if at all possible."[18]

Drysdale learned his lessons well. He led the Dodgers with seventeen wins in 1957 against only nine losses. His earned run average of 2.69 was second in the league behind teammate Johnny Podres. The Dodgers, however, did not fare as well as they had the previous year. They finished in third place, eleven games behind the pennant-winning Milwaukee Braves.

With the season at an end, Drysdale had mixed feelings. The Dodgers had announced they were moving from Brooklyn to Los Angeles. It would be hard for the young pitcher to leave the town he had come to call his second home, its passionate fans, and all the friends he had made there. On the other hand, he was returning to his first home, California.

The Coliseum

In their first four seasons on the West Coast, the Dodgers played their home games in the Los Angeles Coliseum, a football stadium that had been built in the 1920s. The stadium's extremely short left field fence made it a nightmare for pitchers. As Drysdale said in a 1962 interview with *Sports Illustrated*, "A man could hit a ball with his knuckles, and ping! Over the fence she went. I would make a little mistake and that would be all I could think about. I would throw, not pitch and pretty soon I had done another fool thing."[19]

The team opened the season against the Giants in San Francisco, and Drysdale had the honor of pitching the first major-league game played on the West Coast. Unfortunately, he also became the first pitcher to lose a game on the West Coast as Ruben Gomez held the Dodgers scoreless. The Giants won, 8–0.

From there, things went downhill for both Drysdale and the Dodgers. Drysdale lost his first six decisions and couldn't hide his displeasure with the Coliseum and its unusual dimensions. "The Coliseum can't help us pitchers," he told an interviewer. "It's as simple as that. All it can do is put us all in a hole. Most pitchers will get thrown all out of kilter there because they'll have to make adjustments that knock them out of their natural rhythm. Then you go on the road and try to get back in the groove."[20]

Drysdale straightened himself out after the All-Star Game, but it was too late for the Dodgers. They came in seventh in the

Drysdale crosses home plate after hitting his seventh home run of the 1965 season.

National League, ahead of only the hapless Phillies. After winning seventeen games the year before, Drysdale finished with a 12–13 record. The Coliseum did help him in one respect, however. As a batter, he slugged seven home runs for the year, including two in a game against the Braves. The homers enabled him to tie the National League single-season mark held by former teammate Don Newcombe (who had recently been traded to Cincinnati). Drysdale would tie the mark again in 1965, by which time he had established himself as one of the best-hitting pitchers in the game.

Drysdale and the Dodgers both bounced back in 1959. Drysdale again won seventeen games, including four shutouts to tie for the league lead. He also led the league in strikeouts with 242. The team finished in a tie for first with the Braves, forcing a best-of-three play-off. The Dodgers swept the first two games to earn the right to face the Chicago White Sox in the World Series. After losing Game 1, Los Angeles came back to take four of the next five games to win the championship. Drysdale's contribution to the winning effort was a 3–1 victory in Game 3.

The next season, Drysdale's record fell to 15–14. Although he had fewer wins, he actually pitched better than in 1959. His 2.63 earned run average bettered his 1959 mark, as did his five shutouts and league-leading 246 strikeouts. Unfortunately, the team did not support him with many runs, leading to several close defeats.

Because of his improvement, Drysdale's contract for 1961 called for $32,500, a substantial raise of $7,500 over the previous year. On the field, however, he slumped. He won only thirteen games, struck out just 182 batters, and compiled the second-worst earned run average of his career. Drysdale was as disappointed with his performance as anyone. "On this team," he said, "I'm the stopper. When the Dodgers drop a couple of games, I pitch. When we want to get off to a good start in a critical series, I pitch. I'm not supposed to lose."[21]

Drysdale did lead the league in one category in 1961: hit batters. He hit twenty batters with his sidearm deliveries, the highest total in the National League since 1900. It was the fourth straight season he led the league. Drysdale had earned a reputation as an intimidator on the mound, someone who was not afraid to move hitters away from the plate, therefore making it more difficult for them to reach outside pitches. As Huston Horn delicately put it in an article in *Sports Illustrated*, "Some of the people he has hit are fairly certain the element of chance was lacking, and some umpires go along with the thesis."[22] Such was the case that July when he hit Cincinnati Reds outfielder Frank Robinson with a pitch. Drysdale was fined one hundred dollars and suspended for five games for his actions.

When all was said and done, Drysdale was glad to see the 1961 season come to an end. He and his teammates looked forward to leaving the Coliseum and playing in Dodger Stadium in 1962.

A Career Year

The Dodgers' righty-lefty combination of Drysdale and Sandy Koufax would eventually develop into one of the greatest such duos on any pitching staff in major-league history. In 1962, however, Koufax injured his finger and was sidelined from midseason on. Drysdale took on the added burden of trying to replace him and responded with the best year of his career. He won a total of twenty-five games to lead the majors, struck out 232 batters, and had an earned run average of 2.84. He did not miss a turn on the mound, leading National League pitchers in games started for the first of five consecutive years. For his performance, Drysdale received the Cy Young Award, emblematic of pitching supremacy.

Part of Drysdale's effectiveness was due to a change in his pitching delivery. He had always thrown sidearm, which made his pitches extremely difficult for right-handed batters to hit. Lefties, on the other hand, had fewer problems because pitches from a right-hander generally move toward, rather than away, from them. By the end of the 1962 season, he had begun to raise his arm halfway between sidearm and overhand, giving the ball more movement when coming in to left-handed hitters. The results were reflected in his record.

The next season, Drysdale's record dropped to nineteen wins against seventeen losses. His earned run average, however, improved to 2.63. Together with Koufax, he helped the Dodgers to the 1963 pennant. In Game 3 of the World Series, Drysdale stymied the American League–champion Yankees, holding the mighty Bronx Bombers to three hits and no runs. The Dodgers went on to sweep the New Yorkers in four games for their second world championship while representing Los Angeles.

By this point in his career, Drysdale had made the transition from being a thrower to being a pitcher. "I was a smarter pitcher," he explained. "I could pinpoint my offspeed pitches and not depend on my fast ball all the time."[23] Because of this change in pitching philosophy, he was still able to win eighteen games in 1964 even though the Dodgers fell to sixth place in the standings. His earned run average for the year was a career-best 2.19.

The Dodgers returned to the top of the National League standings in 1965 behind the combined pitching of the team's two star hurlers. Drysdale won twenty-three games and lost twelve while Koufax went 26–8. (Drysdale also hit .300, becoming one of the few pitchers to do so in the same year in which they

---

A sidelined Koufax discusses his injured finger with Drysdale in 1962, the best year of Drysdale's career.

won twenty games.) The club's lack of hitting did not hurt it in the World Series where the Dodgers defeated the Minnesota Twins in seven games. After suffering a loss in the opener, Drysdale won Game 4 by a score of 7–2.

The Holdout

The Dodger teams of the early 1960s were built around strong pitching and speed. Koufax and Drysdale could be counted on to keep the team in the game every time they took the mound. Without them, the Dodgers likely would have challenged for last place in the standings.

Following the 1965 season, the two pitchers felt they warranted large raises because of their stellar performances that year. (Koufax had been paid $85,000 for 1965 and Drysdale, $80,000.) When negotiations began for their 1966 contracts, the two teammates learned that general manager Bavasi was trying to play one pitcher against the other in an attempt to keep their salaries down. It was Drysdale's wife, Ginger, who then came up with an idea. "If Buzzie is going to compare the two of you," she said, "why don't you just walk in there together?"[24]

The idea was completely radical for the time. Never before had two players joined forces to negotiate their salaries. Drysdale and Koufax approached Bavasi, requesting a three-year contract, totaling $1 million, to be split evenly between them. Although such salaries do not seem high in today's market, at the time, no pitcher was making over $100,000.

After many meetings between the two sides, the Dodgers still refused to commit to more than one year. The team eventually came around, however, and offered Koufax $125,000 and Drysdale $115,000. Since free agency would not yet come about for several years, the team still held the upper hand. Koufax and Drysdale signed to end their thirty-two-day holdout and reported to the club at the end of spring training.

The Dodgers repeated as National League champs in 1966, with Koufax going 27–9 and winning the Cy Young Award. Drysdale dropped to 13–16 and lost two games in the World Series to the Baltimore Orioles. The Dodgers were swept by the Orioles in what would be Drysdale's final Series appearance.

Drysdale releases the first pitch of the 1965 World Series. The Dodgers defeated the Minnesota Twins in seven games.

The Streak

Koufax retired following the 1966 season because of an arthritic elbow. Without him, Los Angeles dropped to eighth place as Drysdale again compiled a 13–16 record. Some observers began to wonder if he would ever again be the dominant pitcher he had been in the past. With Koufax gone, Drysdale apparently on the downside of his career, and one of the weakest-hitting teams in the league, things did not look good for the Dodgers. Drysdale, however, was not yet finished.

On May 14, Drysdale hurled a 1–0 shutout against the Chicago Cubs. He followed that up with another 1–0 victory four days later against the Houston Astros. Four days after that, he pitched a third consecutive shutout, this time defeating the St. Louis Cardinals and Bob Gibson, 2–0. When he hurled his fourth shutout in a row against the Astros on May 26, the baseball world began to take serious notice.

Drysdale's next start was against the Giants in Dodger Stadium on May 31. With Los Angeles leading 3–0 going into the top of the ninth inning, the Giants loaded the bases with no-body out. With Dick Dietz at the plate, Drysdale threw a pitch that just grazed the batter's elbow. He was set to go to first base, bringing home the runner from third to end Drysdale's streak. Home plate umpire Harry Wendlestedt, however, called him back. Wendlestedt ruled that Dietz had not made an effort to get out of the way of the pitch. He ordered the Giants' catcher to remain at bat, and Dietz finally popped out. When the next two batters were retired without a runner making it home, Drysdale had his fifth consecutive shutout to tie the major-league record. The victory came on the day of the California presidential primary. Drysdale was congratulated by Robert Kennedy in the speech he gave just before he was assassinated by Sirhan Sirhan.

Drysdale added one more shutout to his streak, beating the Pirates on June 4. Four days later, he hurled four more shutout innings against the Phillies before Howie Bedell's sacrifice fly ended his streak. (It was Bedell's only run batted in for the year, and the last of three in his brief career.) Drysdale had thrown fifty-eight-and-two-thirds scoreless innings in a row to break Walter Johnson's major-league mark of fifty-six.

The amazing streak was not enough to save the Dodgers' season. Los Angeles finished in seventh place, twenty-one games behind the Cardinals. Drysdale finished with a 14–12 record, with eight shutouts among his wins. The next year, a torn rotator cuff in his right shoulder forced a premature end to his career. He retired on August 11 as the last active member of the Brooklyn Dodgers. "Drysdale was the heart and soul of the last generation," said teammate Jim Lefebvre. "When he left, an era ended."[25]

The Intimidator

During his career, Drysdale had made numerous appearances on television. Following his retirement, he went into broadcasting, doing play-by-play for the Angels, White Sox, and Dodgers. One of the hardest parts of the job, he said, was doing interviews with the players. "I felt so . . . funny," he explained, "asking players questions when I already knew the answers."[26]

Drysdale wasn't intimidated by the broadcast booth, just as he wasn't intimidated on the mound. He won 209 games in his

Drysdale (top right) displays his plaque after being inducted into the Baseball Hall of Fame in 1984.

career and 3 more in World Series competition. He also pitched in a record eight All-Star Games, compiling a 2–1 mark. Drysdale set a modern National League record by hitting 154 batters in his career. As he once explained his philosophy on knockdown pitches, "If one of our guys went down, I just doubled it. No confusion there. It didn't require a Rhodes scholar."[27]

Drysdale's uniform number 53 was retired by the Dodgers in July 1984. He was inducted into the Baseball Hall of Fame one month later in 1984. In April of 1993, at age fifty-six, he died of a heart attack while in Montreal to announce a game.

CHAPTER 4

Maury Wills

Until 1960, no National League player had stolen 50 or more bases in nearly forty years. That season Maury Wills reached that number with the Dodgers. He followed up by stealing 104 two years later, becoming the first man ever to reach three figures in the category. Wills showed that the stolen base could be an important weapon and helped the Dodgers to the top of the National League standings. He proved to the baseball world that a small man could have just as much of an effect on the outcome of a game as a power hitter or hard-throwing pitcher.

Out of the Projects

Maurice Morning Wills was born on October 2, 1932, in the Anacostia section of Washington, D.C. His parents were the Reverend Guy O. and Mabel Wills. The Wills had thirteen children—eight girls and five boys—with Maury being the seventh in line. To help provide for his large family, his father also worked in the Washington Navy Yard as a machinist.

Life was tough for little Maury, known to his family as Sonny. For much of his childhood, he lived in a cockroach- and

Maury Wills poses in front of a mound of bases in 1962, the year he stole a record-setting 104 bases.

rat-infested apartment in the Parkside projects. With their parents always away working, the Wills children were usually left to take care of themselves. Maury became involved in sports, which helped keep him from engaging in other less-savory activities. He loved baseball but did not have enough money to buy a glove. Instead, he used a paper bag molded into the shape of a mitt.

At Cardozo High School, Maury was a star quarterback on the football team, a guard on the basketball team, and a pitcher who tossed several no-hitters for the baseball team. Although he wasn't a good student, he received several football scholarship offers from major universities. He planned to go to Virginia State University, where his high school coach was going to accept a job.

Before he had the chance, though, he attended a baseball try-out camp run by the New York Giants. Although he fared very well, he was not offered a contract. As he later recalled, "They said there was no such thing as a 155-pound pitcher."[28] The Dodgers, however, were impressed with his speed as a runner and thought he was worth a gamble. He was signed by scout Rex Bowen for a five-hundred-dollar bonus.

A Tour of the Minors

In the spring of 1951, Wills reported to Brooklyn's spring training camp in Vero Beach, Florida. As he later recalled, "When I got to the camp, they had 150 pitchers, three shortstops, two third basemen, and no second baseman."[29] With the odds against him as a pitcher, he decided he would become a second baseman. It would not be until a year later that he was switched to shortstop to take advantage of his strong throwing arm.

Wills began his pro career with the Dodgers' Class D Hornell, New York, club. In succeeding seasons, he moved up to Pueblo in Class A, down to Miami in Class B, and up to Fort Worth in Class AA. When he was sent back to Pueblo in 1955, he gave serious thought to quitting. He realized, however, that he had nothing else to fall back on. "I swallowed my pride and reported to Pueblo," he remembered, "because there was nothing else I could do except play baseball. I made up my mind that I would have a good season and battle my way to the big leagues."[30]

The Majors at Last

Wills batted .302 that season (1956) and led the league in stolen bases. He moved up to Triple A with Seattle of the Pacific Coast League the next year, then over to Spokane for 1958.

Wills's manager at Spokane was Bobby Bragan. Maury had been a right-handed hitter all his life, but Bragan convinced him to try switch-hitting to take advantage of his speed. "Look," he said, "you've got to face the fact that you're never going to play any higher than this unless you learn to be a better hitter. You bat right handed and there are just too many right-handed pitchers around. Why don't you try switch hitting?"[31] Bragan

With his speed and daring on the base paths, Wills (left) proved that the stolen base could be an important offensive weapon.

also helped Wills improve his bunting skills. His advice had a crucial effect on Maury's future.

After eight years in the minors, however, the Dodgers did not hold much hope of him becoming a major leaguer. He was sold to the Detroit Tigers organization, but they returned him to the Dodgers after looking at him in spring training in 1959.

Back at Spokane, Bragan's lessons began to pay off. Wills batted .313 and was finally called up to the majors in midyear. He eventually won the starting shortstop job from Don Zimmer and finished the year with a .260 average in eighty-three games for Los Angeles. His speed and derring-do on the base paths made him an immediate hit with Dodger fans.

A Revolutionary

Ty Cobb of the Detroit Tigers had set the major-league record for stolen bases in a season with ninety-six back in 1915. At that time, speed played an important role in a team's offense. Home runs were at a minimum, and teams often had to manufacture runs by using the hit-and-run, the bunt, and the stolen base. Babe Ruth changed all that in the 1920s. With a livelier ball now in use, Ruth's home runs helped the New York Yankees become the dominant team of the era.

By 1960, the stolen base had become a little-used weapon in most teams' offensive arsenal. Clubs preferred home run hitters who could drive in three or four runs with one swing of the bat. When Wills stole fifty bases to lead the league that year, he became the first National League player to swipe that many since Max Carey stole fifty-one in 1923. (Perhaps even more surprising was Wills's .295 batting average, a good bit higher than his career mark for eight and a half minor-league seasons.) His speed became an important weapon in the Dodgers' attack. It was not unusual to see him work out a walk, steal second base, move to third on a ground out, and score on a sacrifice fly, giving Los Angeles a run without the benefit of a single hit.

Wills's quickness on the base paths caused opposing pitchers to lose their concentration on the mound. They became so worried about the possibility of a steal, they often made poor pitches to the batter at the plate. Rather than throwing curves or other off-speed pitches, they often threw fastballs to prevent him from getting a good jump from first base. This gave the batter an advantage, since fastballs are generally easier to hit, particularly when a batter is expecting one. When balls were hit, Wills's speed caused opposing fielders to rush their throws in an effort to keep him from taking an extra base.

In 1961, Wills won another stolen base title, this time with a total of thirty-five. No one was prepared, however, for what would occur in 1962.

An Amazing Record

As much time as Wills had put into improving his hitting, he put just as much into becoming an even better base runner. He studied every pitcher to get the best jump off first base. He paid attention to the positioning of the infielders and tried to get the catcher's signs so he would know on which pitch to run. In 1962, all his efforts were rewarded as he put together a season beyond everyone's wildest expectations.

Wills got off to a fast start stealing bases in 1962 and never slowed down. On September 7, he stole four against the Pirates to break Bob Bescher's fifty-one-year-old National League record of eighty-one. Just over two weeks later, he tied Cobb's long-standing major-league mark of ninety-six by stealing second base in the third inning of a game against the Cardinals. He broke the record six innings later.

Wills added seven more steals before the season was over, giving him the incredible total of 104. Such was his ability on the base paths, he undoubtedly could have stolen even more. As he would say in later years, "I'll always regret that I didn't try to steal more. . . . I probably could have stolen 125 had I gone for everything in sight. I had plenty of opportunities to steal when the club had a comfortable lead but I passed them up."[32] It was an unwritten rule of the day that a team did not try to run up a score when it had a substantial lead.

Wills's running was vital to the Dodgers' success that year, helping to keep them in the pennant race until the end of the season. He could not win the pennant all by himself, however.

Wills dives headfirst into second base as he steals his ninety-sixth base of the 1962 season.

Despite his three steals in Game 3 of the play-off series with the Giants, San Francisco came from behind in the eighth inning to take the game and the National League flag.

In addition to his steals, Wills also collected 208 base hits including a league-leading ten triples. He batted .299 and won a Gold Glove for his fielding excellence. For his performance, Wills was named the Most Valuable Player of the National League. He also won the Hickock Belt as the Professional Athlete of the Year.

Stolen Base King

All the sliding, quick starts, and quick stops involved in stealing so many bases in 1962 took a toll on Wills's legs. It got to the point where he had to receive hypnotic treatment to ignore the constant pain that he felt. The aches and pains limited his effectiveness the following season. After further injuring his foot on opening day, he stole just forty bases in 1963, a total still good enough to lead the league. He continued to improve as a hitter, however, and raised his average to .302. Wills followed up with fifty-three more steals in 1964 to lead the National League for the fifth consecutive year. While Wills continued to spark the Dodgers with his play, the rest of the team struggled. Los Angeles finished in sixth place in 1964, and prospects for the next season did not look good.

With his foot completely healed, Wills broke from the gate

Wills's aggressive base running took a serious toll on his legs.

quickly in 1965, pilfering five bases in his first two games. By the halfway point of the season, he had forty-nine steals and was threatening to make a run at his record. His running helped the Dodgers reach first place, where they would remain for the rest of the season. Joe Reichler elaborated on Wills's importance to the team in a series of articles he penned for the Associated Press. "Wills has probably contributed more than anyone else to the team's cause," wrote Reichler. "First, he plays in just about every game and reaches base at an unmatched rate. But it is his breathtaking exploits on the basepaths that have captivated baseball fans throughout the National League. At an age when he should be slowing up, Wills appears to be faster and more daring than ever before."[33]

Wills finished the year with ninety-four steals, leading the league for the sixth—and final—time. In Game 5 of the World Series against the Twins, he tied a Series record by getting four hits, including a pair of doubles. He batted .367 for the Series and stole three bases to help the Dodgers to their third championship on the West Coast.

Goodbye Los Angeles

After his standout 1965 season, Wills held out for more money and eventually signed a new contract for $85,000. However, at the age of thirty-three, his body was finally showing signs of wearing down. He stole just thirty-eight bases in 1966 and failed to lead the league for the first time since his rookie season. The Dodgers again won the National League pennant, but were swept in the World Series by the Baltimore Orioles.

Following the Series, the Dodgers were scheduled to travel to Japan to play a series of exhibition games. Wills's right knee had been bothering him, and he requested permission to skip the trip. When the Japanese promoters threatened to cancel the tour, however, general manager Buzzie Bavasi said he would have to go but would not be required to play.

Nevertheless, when the team arrived in Japan, Wills was inserted into the lineup. After reinjuring his knee, Wills asked for permission to return home. When owner Walter O'Malley refused, Wills left on his own. Infuriated, O'Malley traded him to the Pittsburgh Pirates less than one month later.

From Player to Manager to Addict

Wills was Pittsburgh's regular shortstop for two seasons. In 1967 he tied his career high with a batting average of .302, but stole only twenty-nine bases. The next year, he finished second in the league in steals with fifty-two. At age thirty-six, however, he was left unprotected in the expansion draft. He was claimed by the new Montreal Expos franchise, but was traded back to the Dodgers in mid-1969. Wills was the team's regular shortstop for two more seasons, but lost his job to Bill Russell in 1972. That year, Wills was released after batting just .129 in seventy-one games. He ended his fourteen-year big-league career with a lifetime batting average of .281 and 586 stolen bases.

Wills and Pittsburgh Pirates teammate Willie Stargell in 1968.

Following his playing career, Wills landed a job as a baseball broadcaster for NBC television. He still had his heart set, however, on returning to the major leagues. Since 1970, he had spent the winter seasons managing a team in the Mexican leagues. A decade later, he was hired by the Seattle Mariners to replace Darrell Johnson and become the third black manager in major-league history.

Unfortunately, Wills was not as successful as a manager as he had been as a player. He directed the hapless Mariners to just twenty wins in their last fifty-eight games of the 1980 season. The team finished in last place in the Western Division of the American League in their fourth season of existence.

Wills began the next season looking forward to improvement, but the team failed to respond. Prior to an early season game against the Oakland Athletics in Seattle, Oakland manager Billy Martin noticed something strange about the batters' boxes. When umpire Bill Kunkel measured them, they were found to be a foot too long. Wills had instructed the grounds crew to extend the lines in an attempt to give his players an advantage. (If the Mariner batters moved up farther in the box, they could reach the curveballs thrown by Oakland pitchers before they had a chance to break.) Wills thought his action was blown out of proportion. "That's not cheating," he said, "just a little gamesmanship."[34] The league thought otherwise: Wills was suspended two games and fined five hundred dollars.

The embarrassing incident added to the team's problems. After twenty-four games, the Mariners had won just six. Deciding a change had to be made, they fired Wills and replaced him with Rene Lachemann. By this time, pressures on and off the field had caused Wills to become heavily involved with alcohol and drugs. As he wrote in his 1991 autobiography, *On the Run*, "In 3 1/2 years, I spent more than $1,000,000 of my own money on cocaine."[35] The former All-Star's life was quickly spinning out of control.

The Road Back

By the mid-1980s, Wills had sunk as low as he possibly could. He had tried to get help for his alcohol and drug problems as early as 1983, but it was not until five years later that he finally stopped using. With the help of former Dodger pitcher Don Newcombe, he began attending therapy classes and joined Alcoholics Anonymous. The road back was not an easy one, but Wills eventually shook his habit.

Today, Wills is the Dodgers' minor-league bunting and baserunning coordinator. He also spends much of his time traveling around the country talking to young people about the dangers of drugs. He is involved with the Red Ribbon Program, a national organization whose goal is to promote a healthy and drug-free lifestyle. Wills is proud of his work and continues to try to be a positive influence in the lives of youngsters around the country. As he has said, "I am proud to be a role model to

Wills throws the opening pitch at Dodger Stadium in 2001. The former Dodger shortstop has successfully battled alcohol and drug addiction.

children and aspiring athletes. I feel it is my obligation to give back something to this community that has done so much for me. If I can accomplish this, then I feel I have truly realized my greatest victory."[36]

Wills's victories on the field of play included helping to usher in a new era by once again making the stolen base an important offensive weapon. In the early 1960s, he was the key figure in the Dodgers' attack. Wills led the National League in stolen bases six years in a row, and compiled 586 for his career. He blazed a path that stars like Lou Brock and Rickey Henderson would follow in years to come.

CHAPTER 5

Steve Garvey

Steve Garvey was one of the most durable players of his era, once playing in a National League–record 1,207 consecutive games. He was part of baseball's longest-running infield with the Dodgers, combining superior baseball skills with a reputation for being the all-American boy. Garvey is remembered today as being one of the great clutch hitters of his time but, more important, as someone who respected his team, the game, and the fans who paid his salary.

Born to Be a Dodger

Steven Patrick Garvey was born on December 22, 1948, in Tampa, Florida. His mother, Mildred, was a secretary at an insurance company, and his father, Joe, was a bus driver. Both of his parents were originally from Long Island. When his mother was a little girl, her mother was the victim of a freak accident that left her with neurological problems. These problems became worse as she got older until doctors finally said it would be in her best interest to move to the warmer climate of the South. Steve's parents decided to go along to be near his grandparents. They arrived in Tampa about a month before he was born.

Steve enjoyed his childhood in Tampa. "Tampa was a wonderful place to grow up," he remembered. "You don't have the complexities of a real metropolitan area like Chicago, New York or Los Angeles. It's simpler there, more age-appropriate for kids. It's a slower pace, much more family-oriented. I loved Tampa."[37] As a young boy, one of Steve's responsibilities was to go to his grandmother's house after school and help out with the chores. If he had time after he finished, he would play with his friends. He was active in basketball, football, and golf, but his favorite sport of all was baseball. Since his grandfather was originally from Brooklyn, it was only natural that the Dodgers were his favorite team.

The young Steve Garvey was inspired by Dodgers first baseman Gil Hodges (pictured).

When Steve was seven years old, his father began driving a bus for the Dodgers during spring training. Steve would often tag along and act as batboy for the team. He noticed the way the players acted and how they treated the fans. His favorite was first baseman Gil Hodges. Hodges made a strong impression on the youngster. He admired the way he was respected by the other players and how he always had time for the fans. He would remember this in later years and try to act the same way when he was in similar situations. As he later said, "The time [I] spent with the Dodgers made baseball seem very wonderful to me. I sincerely think I was born to be a Dodger."[38]

A Future Star

Steve did well in both Little League ball and in junior high. At Chamberlain High School, however, his talent really began to shine through. He made the baseball, football, and basketball teams at Chamberlain and played a position of leadership in each sport. "In football," he recalled, "I was the quarterback, making plays and scoring. In basketball, I was the play-making guard. In baseball, I moved to shortstop and also did some pitching."[39]

In Steve's junior year, he batted .475. He hit .465 as a senior to win the county batting title. He was named to the all-city and all-conference teams for three consecutive years. College recruiters came knocking at his door. Although he was selected by the Minnesota Twins in the annual baseball draft, he decided instead to accept a baseball scholarship to Michigan State University in East Lansing. Although he dreamed of becoming a major-league player, his more realistic goals were to become a baseball coach and teacher.

At Michigan State, Steve played defensive back in football and third base on the baseball team. His baseball coach, former major leaguer Danny Litwhiler, knew he had the makings of a special player. "Steve was an awesome hitter in college," he recalled. "He hit towering home runs. But it was his mental toughness that was so impressive. . . . My only question about his making it was his defense. . . . He was acceptable at third, but no more than that."[40] Garvey hit .450 as a freshman and .383 as a sophomore. In 1983, the Dodgers selected him in the June draft and signed him to a package worth fifty thousand dollars—forty thousand dollars in cash and ten thousand dollars to finish his education at Michigan State.

A Dream Come True

Garvey began his pro career with Ogden, Utah, of the Class A Pioneer League. As a rookie, he batted .338 for the championship team and led the league with twenty home runs. However, having suffered a separated shoulder in college, his arm was still giving him some problems. He struggled in the field and led all third basemen in errors with twenty-three.

The next year, Garvey was promoted to Albuquerque of the Texas League. After injuring a hamstring while running out a hit, he was put at first base so he could remain in the lineup. It was his first time playing the position, and he found that he liked it. However, since the Dodgers already had a Gold Glove (an award given to the best fielder at each position) player at first base on the major-league team in the person of Wes Parker, Garvey knew his future was at third base. He returned there after his leg healed but continued to struggle in the field. At the plate, however, he had no problems, hitting .373.

On September 1 of each year, major-league teams are allowed to expand their rosters and bring up their most promising minor-league players. Garvey was recalled by the Dodgers and made his debut on September 1, 1969. The next year, he batted .350 in spring training and won the third base job with the major-league club. He struggled at the plate when the regular season began, however, and was soon sent down to Spokane. Although Garvey was depressed at the setback, his father helped him put things in perspective. "Listen, we know you've given a hundred percent," he told him. "You haven't let anybody down. Baseball's always been fun for you, so go down there and have fun. Everything is going to be fine."[41]

Garvey regained his batting stroke in the minors and batted over .300 when he was recalled in September. He stuck with the big-league team in 1971, but a broken bone in his hand hindered his progress. Limited to eighty-one games, he batted just .227 with seven home runs and twenty-six runs batted in (RBIs).

The next year, Garvey raised his average to .269, but hit just nine homers and drove in but thirty runs. He continued to be plagued by problems in the field. He led National League third basemen in errors, most of them coming on bad throws. The Dodgers began to look at Ron Cey at third base, and rumors circulated that Garvey might be traded away.

Despite his struggles, Garvey continued to show glimpses of his great potential, and the club was hesitant to let him go. He began to have self-doubts, wondering if he would ever fulfill that potential. His wife, Cyndy, whom he had married following the 1971 season, would not let him get down on himself. "You've never been a quitter," she told him. "Don't start now."[42]

A portrait of Garvey in 1971. Garvey struggled at third base during his early years as a Dodger before finding success as a first baseman.

Finally, in June 1973, manager Walt Alston put Garvey at first base for the second game of a doubleheader. (By this time, Parker had retired.) He responded by getting two hits. From that point on, his hitting kept him in the lineup as the Dodgers' first baseman.

Steve Garvey, All-Star

Garvey batted .306 in 1973, an improvement of nearly forty points over his average of the previous season. He did not take success for granted, however, embracing every opportunity to discuss hitting with other players and coaches. One of those most responsible for helping him improve as a hitter was Dodgers coach Dixie Walker. Walker worked with him on hitting to the opposite field with more authority and on hitting down on the ball to prevent uppercutting (swinging up at the ball, which often results in pop-ups or strikeouts).

In 1974, Garvey put all that he had learned into practice and the results were impressive. By the midway point in the season, he was up among the league leaders in batting average, home runs, and runs batted in. In the voting for the All-Star Game, he was elected by the fans as the starting first baseman as a write-in candidate. (The names of only eight first basemen were listed on the printed ballot.) In storybook fashion, Garvey got two hits and was named the game's Most Valuable Player.

Garvey finished the year with twenty-one home runs, 111 runs batted in, and a .312 average. His .389 average in the National League Championship Series against the Pirates earned him another MVP trophy. In the World Series that fall, he batted .381, but it was not enough to keep Los Angeles from losing to the Oakland Athletics in five games. Garvey completed a rare triple by being named the National League's Most Valuable Player for the year to go with his other two MVP awards. He capped off his season by winning a Gold Glove Award as the league's best-fielding first baseman. (Garvey's fielding was much better than it had been at third. Many of his errors at third were made on bad throws. A first baseman has far fewer throws to make.)

The 1974 season also marked the beginning of a remarkable run for Los Angeles. Garvey at first base was joined in the Dodgers infield by Davey Lopes at second base, Cey at third base, and Bill Russell at shortstop. The quartet would remain together as a unit through 1981, longer than any other infield in major-league history.

Mr. Clean

During the 1974 season, Garvey began to become more involved in the Los Angeles community. He appreciated his good fortune in being able to earn a good living playing baseball and wanted to give something back to the fans who supported him. Garvey gave his time to causes such as multiple sclerosis, muscular dystrophy, and abused children. He made public service announcements, visited hospitals, and did what he could to raise money. His work with these charities helped make him more and more popular with the fans. As former teammate Bill Buckner said, "He was a natural with the public; he always did the right thing at the right time, and the people took a liking to him."[43]

For his good works and clean-cut image, Garvey was viewed as the all-American boy. As former manager Tommy

Lasorda said, "He was always respectful and an outstanding young man. He never showed me one moment of disrespect and he was a fantastic role model. I never saw him refuse a kid an autograph."[44]

Unfortunately, several of Garvey's teammates on the Dodgers felt much of what he did was an act. They resented the

Garvey with Johnny Carson on The Tonight Show *in 1978. Garvey's good looks and charisma made him popular with the public and media.*

attention he and his wife Cyndy received. The first time this resentment surfaced was in 1975. Garvey did not let tension in the clubhouse affect his performance on the field, however. He had another excellent season, collecting 210 hits and batting .319. The Dodgers finished in second place, twenty games behind the powerful Cincinnati Reds' "Big Red Machine." The team followed the same script in 1976. They again finished second to Cincinnati despite another solid season by Garvey.

Prior to the 1977 season, Garvey was rewarded with a new six-year, $2 million contract. Tommy Lasorda took over the managerial reins from Walter Alston, and the Dodgers responded by winning the National League pennant. Garvey played a key role, setting career highs in both home runs (33) and runs batted in (115) while batting .297. Toward the end of the season, he received a tribute of another kind: Lindsay Junior High School in central California was renamed Steve Garvey Junior High School in his honor.

Ups and Downs

Garvey continued to be a solid offensive force with the Dodgers over the next five seasons. Playing day in and day out, he batted over .300 three times, led the league in hits twice, and drove in more than one hundred runs three times. In 1978, he was named Most Valuable Player of the All-Star Game for the second time. Three years later he won his first—and only— championship ring when the Dodgers defeated the New York Yankees in six games in the World Series.

Not all the times were good ones, however. In 1978 he had a widely publicized clubhouse confrontation with pitcher Don Sutton, who had made critical remarks about Garvey. When Sutton brought up Cyndy Garvey's name, the discussion led to a scuffle, and the two players had to be separated. Neither Garvey nor Sutton was seriously hurt, but the situation added to the tensions in the clubhouse.

Two years later, the Garveys were interviewed for an article in *Inside Sports* magazine. The article, titled "Trouble in Paradise," painted a very negative picture of the couple. The Garveys sued the magazine and eventually settled out of court. (Their marriage would end in divorce three years later.)

Perhaps the most surprising event of all was Garvey's split with the Dodgers. With his contract up following the 1982 season, Garvey sought a new five-year pact to ensure that he would finish his career with the team. When the Dodgers refused to offer more than three years, he filed for free agency. That December, he signed a five-year, $6.6 million contract with the San Diego Padres. Garvey's long association with the Dodgers had come to an end.

Life After Los Angeles

Some of Garvey's teammates resented all the attention that was paid to Garvey and his wife, Cyndy.

In five years with San Diego, Garvey provided the Padres with the veteran leadership they had been lacking. Said utility infielder Tim Flannery, "Just having a guy like him in the lineup gives you confidence. You see the way he does the little things that are so big—moving runners from first to second, getting that sacrifice fly in the last inning. And when it comes down to the game situation with the winning run on second and two outs, the guy you want up is Steve."[45]

San Diego finished fourth in Garvey's first season, but he passed a significant milestone along the way. Early in the year, he played in his 1,118th consecutive game to break Billy Williams's National League record. The mark was especially gratifying to Garvey. It meant he could be counted on to play day in and day out, through any illnesses, injuries, or slumps. This was extremely important to someone who had been taught as a child to finish what he started. He would eventually extend the record to 1,207 games before a dislocated thumb kept him out of the second game of a doubleheader on July 29, 1983.

In 1984, the Padres won the National League Western Division crown. At age thirty-five, Garvey was not as productive as he had been earlier in his career. However, he still provided the most dramatic moment of the National League Championship Series against the Chicago Cubs. With Chicago leading two games to one, Garvey's two-run game-winning home run in the bottom of the ninth inning in Game 4 evened the series at two games apiece. Garvey recalled the moment vividly. "As soon as the ball went toward the fence," he said, "everything froze in time. It was as if all sound stopped."[46] The home run capped an outstanding day for the first baseman. In addition to the two-run blast, he also stroked two singles and a double and brought home three other runs. With the momentum having turned in their favor, the Padres went on to win the deciding game to reach the World Series for the first time in franchise history.

Garvey tags a runner at first during the 1984 National League Championship Series between the San Diego Padres and the Chicago Cubs.

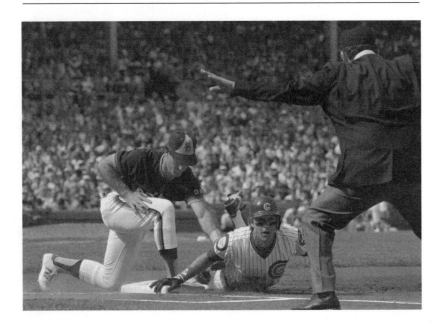

Garvey played three more years with the Padres, retiring after the 1987 season. His career totals include 2,599 hits, 272 home runs, 1,308 runs batted in, and a .294 batting average. In ten All-Star Games, he batted .393 with a slugging average of .955. His ability to hit in the clutch resulted in National League Championship Series career records for home runs (8) and runs batted in (24).

Since his retirement, Garvey has continued to devote much of his time to charity. He also runs the Steve Garvey Management Group and gives motivational speeches around the country. His political ambitions were put on hold when he was named in two paternity suits, but he does not rule out running for office in the future. Although his Mr. Clean image was tarnished, Garvey remains admired for his dedication, hard work, and love of the game of baseball.

CHAPTER 6

Tommy Lasorda

Tommy Lasorda summed up his baseball outlook in no uncertain terms. "I bleed Dodger blue," he said, "and when I
die, I'm going to the Big Dodger in the sky."[47] Following a brief
career as a pitcher, he brought his enthusiasm, love of the game,
and ability to motivate players to the field of managing. The results included eight West Division championships, four National League pennants, and two world championships in
twenty seasons at the helm of the team he loved.

Keeping the Dream

Thomas Charles Lasorda, the second of Sabatino and
Carmella Lasorda's five boys, was born on September 22,
1927, in Norristown, Pennsylvania. Sabatino was an Italian
immigrant who drove a truck at the Bethlehem Steel quarry
in Norristown. He considered himself extremely lucky to be
living in America and conveyed his zest for life and love of
people to everyone he met. At the same time, however, he
was a strict disciplinarian with his children. As Tommy re-
lated in later years, "I kissed my father, Sam, every time I
saw him until the day he died. His five sons would have

Tommy Lasorda spent twenty seasons as manager of his beloved Los Angeles Dodgers.

gone through fire for him. But if we got out of line, the roof fell in."[48]

Although the Lasorda family was poor, they never lacked love and affection. As Tommy wrote in his autobiography, "The house was always filled with people and laughter and singing."[49] Since all of the boys enjoyed eating, it was sometimes difficult putting enough food on the table. To try to help make ends meet, the family grew much of its own food on a small vegetable patch a few miles from their home. Tommy did everything he could to help bring in money, including shoveling snow, shining shoes, and delivering potatoes.

As a youngster, Lasorda's love of baseball helped keep him out of trouble. He practiced whenever he could and dreamed of someday playing in Yankee Stadium in New York. Unfortunately, as a member of the Norristown High School baseball team, he was no more than a third-string pitcher. Each of his pitches was nothing more than average, but his desire could not be matched.

Although Tommy did not pitch much for his high school team, he did start for the Norristown Parks and Recreation

League All-Stars. From there he moved on to the Connie Mack All-Stars, a team composed of the best young players in the Philadelphia area. While in Philadelphia, he attracted the interest of Phillies' scout Jocko Collins. Collins must have seen something that Tommy's high school coach had missed. The Phillies signed him to a minor-league contract before the end of his senior year when he was just sixteen years old. The fact that he would receive one hundred dollars a month was a bonus to the youngster. As he later told the scout, "If you'd waited five minutes more, I would've offered you $200 a month to let me play professional baseball."[50] Lasorda dropped out of school before graduating and began his pro career in 1945 with Concord of the North Carolina State League.

The Road to the Majors

Lasorda compiled a 3–12 record for Concord in 1945, then entered the military service for two years. When he returned in 1948, he joined the Schenectady club of the Class C Canadian-American League. He pitched a few noteworthy games that season. He set a league record by striking out twenty-five Amsterdam Rugmakers in a fifteen-inning contest, then followed it up by fanning fifteen and thirteen in his next two games. His total of fifty-three strikeouts in three games was also a league mark.

Despite these bright moments, Tommy's record for the year was just 9–12 as he was plagued by control problems. Depressed by his mediocre performance, he called his father for advice. "I never taught you how to quit," said the elder Lasorda, "and if you're gonna quit on yourself you might as well come home right now."[51]

Lasorda listened to his father and decided to finish the season. However, after the season, he was left unprotected by the Phillies. The Brooklyn Dodgers drafted him in November for four thousand dollars. He was assigned to Greenville of the Class A Sally League. He posted a 7–7 record there in 1949 and was promoted to the Dodgers' Montreal farm club of the Triple A International League the next season. It was the beginning of a lifetime love affair. "From the day I signed with Montreal," he later recalled, "I'd known the Dodger organization was for me."[52]

Lasorda eventually would spend a total of nine years in Montreal. He was called up to the big-league club for the first time in 1954. He pitched in only four games that year without a win or loss.

The next spring, brimming with confidence, the brash Lasorda announced, "I don't intend to let anyone push me off this club, regardless of the record he has."[53] After two relief appearances, he made his first start on May 5 against the St. Louis Cardinals at Ebbets Field. He lasted just one inning, but it was enough to put him in the record books. He tied a major-league mark by throwing three wild pitches in a single frame. To add insult to injury (or injury to insult), he was spiked by the Cardinals' Wally Moon on a play at the plate and was forced to leave the game. Lasorda made one more disastrous appearance after coming back from the disabled list. Soon after, he was told he was being returned to Montreal. The Dodgers had to make room on their roster for a young man by the name of Sandy Koufax.

During spring training the next year, the Dodgers sold Lasorda's contract to the Kansas City Athletics. "We think the world of you, Tom," said general manager Buzzie Bavasi, "and there'll be a place for you any time you want to come back to the Dodgers. But we had this chance to sell you and we didn't want to deny you the opportunity to pitch in the majors. You've worked too hard to earn it."[54]

Lasorda pitched in eighteen games for the Athletics in 1956, compiling a 0–4 record. He struck out twenty-eight batters in his forty-five innings of work, but walked forty-five. His earned run average was an unimpressive 6.20. He was traded to the Yankees in midseason and finished the year with their Denver farm team in the American Association.

The Making of a Manager

By this point, as he was approaching his thirtieth birthday, Lasorda realized a career as a major-league pitcher might not be in his future. He remembered Buzzie Bavasi's words and decided his best chance to remain in baseball was with the Dodgers' organization. The Yankees agreed to help and sold him to Brooklyn in May 1957. After playing that year with the team's Los Angeles club in the Pacific Coast League, he

Lasorda in 1956 during his short-lived career as a pitcher for the Kansas City Athletics.

returned to Montreal for three more seasons.

With Montreal, Lasorda served as a player-coach and also acted as the club's traveling secretary. In 1958, his first year serving in all three capacities, the team won the International League championship. Lasorda had the best season of his pro career, winning eighteen games with an earned run average of 2.50. He also made the All-Star team and was named the league's Pitcher of the Year. In recognition of his performance and of his years in Montreal, the team honored him with Tom Lasorda Day on August 23. Two years later, in July 1960, Lasorda retired as the International League's all-time leader in career wins with 107. Shortly thereafter, he was signed by the Dodgers as a scout.

In November 1962, five years after the Dodgers had relocated to Los Angeles, Lasorda was asked to move his base of operations from Pennsylvania to California. He continued learning under general manager Al Campanis and remained a full-time scout until 1965. That year, he got his first shot at managing with the Dodgers' Pocatello Chiefs farm team. He brought the club home in second place, then moved on to the Ogden Dodgers of the Pioneer League. There, he won pennants in each of his three seasons (1966–1968). Advancing up the ladder to Triple-A, he won pennants with the Spokane Indians in 1970 (when he was named Minor League Manager of the Year) and with the Albuquerque Dukes two years later.

Right from the beginning, Lasorda's managerial style was confrontational. In his very first game at Pocatello, his team loaded the bases with nobody out in the first inning. The next batter tapped a foul ball that Lasorda handled from his position in the coaches' box behind third base. He examined the ball and threw it out of play for being dirty. The opposing manager, however, took issue with him. One word led to another and within minutes, the two men were racing toward each other. Lasorda dropped his counterpart with a single punch and both dugouts emptied. The melee was finally broken up by the police. As Lasorda explained in an interview for *New Times*, "I had a small man's complex, I guess you'd call it, when I was a player and started as a manager, and I got into so many fights."[55] His explosive temper got him ejected from roughly one out of every five games.

Despite his aggressive managerial style, in 1973 Lasorda was called up to serve as third-base coach with the major-league club. He remained with the team in that capacity until being named to succeed Walter Alston as manager in September of 1976. It was a position he would hold for twenty seasons.

The Master Motivator

Lasorda's style was in direct contrast to that of the man he succeeded. As *Sports Illustrated*'s Larry Keith reported from spring training in 1977, "Florida was quite different from what it had been for two decades. The man in charge was moving here, hurrying there, shouting orders, giving directions, laughing, talking a mile a minute, cajoling, and praising."[56] The Dodgers responded to his cheerleading and ran away with the National League West title that year. They defeated the Phillies to take the pennant, but lost to the Yankees in the World Series. Lasorda was named the National League Manager of the Year by both United Press International and the Associated Press as nearly 3 million fans came out to Dodger Stadium to see the team play.

Lasorda (right) replaced Walter Alston (left) when Alston retired in 1976 after twenty-three years as manager of the Dodgers.

The Dodgers repeated their success in 1978, again winning the pennant and again losing the Series to New York. After a two-year break, they again won the pennant in the strike-shortened 1981 season. This time the Dodgers defeated the Yankees in the Series, giving Lasorda his first championship. Of his team, Lasorda later said, "They were tremendous guys. They loved to play. And, boy, they believed in themselves. The Yankees had beat us in two World Series. Then we played the mighty Yankees again, and we were two games down, and they figured we couldn't bounce back. And we beat them four straight."[57]

Over the next four years, Los Angeles won two more divisional titles but could not get past the National League Championship Series. The team's loss to the St. Louis Cardinals in 1985 was especially hard to take. The key blow in the final game was a game-winning three-run home run by St. Louis slugger Jack Clark, who many observers thought should have been walked intentionally. Because of this, many fans and members of the media questioned Lasorda's managerial skills. Lasorda accepted the blame. He insisted he made the right move and refused to allow the setback to demoralize the team. "We'll be back," he told reporters. "We'll be back. You can count on it, we'll be back."[58]

The Dodgers finished out of contention in the next two seasons but bounced back to take the National League West crown in 1988. Led by right-hander Orel Hershiser, they proceeded to upset the heavily favored New York Mets in the League Championship Series. "They had beaten us 10 of 11 times that year," recalled Lasorda. "The 12th game was rained out. So nobody, and I mean nobody, gave us a chance."[59]

Playing Oakland in the World Series, the Dodgers continued to perform their magic. In Game 1, they came from behind to win on a dramatic ninth-inning home run by injured pinch hitter Kirk Gibson. "It was just plain magic," remembered outfielder Mickey Hatcher. "We send a cripple up there in a wheelchair, and he hits a home run to win a World Series game. I mean, come on."[60]

Spurred by the startling blow, Los Angeles went on to defeat the Athletics in five games to give Lasorda his second championship ring. As sportswriter Mike Lupica wrote in a piece for *Esquire*, "Lasorda beat the mighty A's in 1988 with a team that didn't belong anywhere near October. It was one of the finest managing jobs ever."[61]

"Bigger Than the World Series"

From 1989 through 1996, Lasorda's Dodgers won two more West Division titles (1994 and 1995). He enhanced his reputation as one of the greatest managers of the day and one of the greatest motivators of all time. A classic example of his ability to rally his troops occurred in Game 4 of the 1988 Series when NBC broadcaster Bob Costas called the Dodgers' starting lineup perhaps the weakest in World Series history. Lasorda got his team so outraged by the innocent remark, opposing manager Tony LaRussa himself became concerned about the Dodgers' emotional edge. Los Angeles won Games 4 and 5 to stun the heavily favored Athletics. Lasorda's explanation of his success was simple. "I motivate players through communication, being honest with them, having them respect and appreciate your ability and your help," he said.[62]

Lasorda compiled a record of 1,599 wins and 1,439 losses in twenty years at the helm before being forced to retire because of a heart attack in 1996. "I was getting tired really fast," he later said, "and there was no way I was going to go back if I

Lasorda proudly served as manager of the gold medal–winning United States Olympic Baseball Team in 2000.

couldn't manage the way I wanted to. I didn't know if I could go through the effort it would have taken because I have to manage with a great deal of enthusiasm and a lot of excitement. I couldn't do it any other way."[63]

After stepping down as manager, Lasorda was named senior vice president of the Dodgers. He was elected to the Baseball Hall of Fame in 1997 in recognition of his eight Western Division championships, four National League pennants, and two World Series titles. One of his greatest moments in baseball, however, was yet to come.

As both a player and manager, Lasorda had traveled to many countries. He spread the gospel of baseball to Cuba, Puerto Rico, and the Dominican Republic during his years playing winter ball. In 2000, he received another opportunity to promote his love for the sport on the international stage when he was named manager of the U.S. Olympic Baseball Team.

Lasorda took a group of twenty-four minor-league players to Sydney, Australia. There, they proceeded to stun the world by defeating the heavily favored Cuban team in the final game. It was the crowning achievement in Lasorda's near half-century of involvement with the game. After the Americans' 4–0 victory that won them the gold medal, he proclaimed, "This is bigger than the World Series! This is bigger than the Dodgers! This is bigger than Major League Baseball!"[64]

CHAPTER 7

Fernando Valenzuela

Few rookies have broken onto the major-league scene the way pitcher Fernando Valenzuela did in 1981. He won his first eight starts that year, hurling five shutouts in the process. The Mexican native inspired a national phenomenon ("Fernando-mania") and became a hero among his countrymen in a major-league career that covered seventeen seasons and saw him win 173 games. His devastating screwball and excellent control made him one of the top pitchers of his day.

Life in Etchohuaquila

Fernando Anguamea Valenzuela was the youngest of twelve children born to Avelino and Hermenegilda Anguamea de Valenzuela. He was born in the tiny (population 150) village of Etchohuaquila in Sonora, Mexico, on November 1, 1960. Fernando's father was a farmer who grew garbanzo beans, sunflowers, and corn on a few acres of farmland behind his home under a government program.

The Valenzuela family was very poor. Their four-room, thatch-roofed, adobe hut originally belonged to Fernando's grandfather. It did not have running water or electricity. To

86

bring in some extra money, the older boys worked the nearby fields on property owned by rich ranchers.

Like nearly all Mexican boys, Fernando loved both baseball and soccer. Although he was bright, he quit school in the sixth grade and spent all of his time playing sports. He eventually stuck with baseball because his talent, he said, was in his hands rather than in his feet.

As a youngster, Fernando played first base for the Etchohuaquila town team. His brothers Rafael, Francisco, Daniel, Gerardo, Manuel de Jesus, and Avelino also played on the team. "My brother Rafael was the first one who told me I could play baseball professionally," said Fernando. "He had played pro ball himself, so he knew. He gave me confidence."[65]

Left-handed Mexican pitching sensation Fernando Valenzuela in 1982.

As Fernando got older, he decided he wanted to be a pitcher. In 1976, when he was fifteen, he was given the opportunity to pitch in a tournament for the Navojoa all-star team. His family was so poor, he did not have his own glove. He had to borrow a right-hander's glove even though he threw left-handed. It didn't seem to affect his pitching, however. He won three games as a reliever in the tournament and led the team to the state championship. In the championship series, he was voted Most Valuable Player.

When Fernando returned home, he was contacted by the general manager of the Navojoa Mayos and offered $250 to play winter ball. He accepted but did not see much action as a pitcher because of his young age. He did learn much, however, by observing the older players.

The following spring, Fernando was signed by the Puebla Angels, who loaned him to the Guanajuato club of the minor-league Mexican Center League. He compiled a 6–9 record in 1978 but showed promise by striking out ninety-one batters in

Valenzuela impressed Dodgers' scouts with his excellent control and curveball.

ninety-six innings. The next year he moved up to the Yucatan Lions of the Mexican League (Mexico's major league). He was named the league's Rookie of the Year despite winning just ten games against twelve losses.

Playing pro ball helped the youngster grow up quickly. He was away from home for much of the time and had to learn to take care of himself. He enjoyed the life of a ballplayer and began to put on weight and add girth to his frame.

Around this time, Fernando caught the attention of a scout named Corito Varona. Varona suggested the Dodgers take a look at the portly youngster. As it so happened, Dodgers' scout Mike Brito was in the area to look at a shortstop prospect. He did not think the shortstop had the talent to make it to the majors, but he was impressed by the pitcher who threw against the youngster's team. That pitcher was Valenzuela. As Brito later reported, "He had such good movement and location of his fastball, and a curve he threw three-quarters and overhand. He kept the ball low, and he was cool. Twice the other team had the bases loaded in that game and he struck out the side."[66]

Brito told general manager Al Campanis about Valenzuela, and Campanis came down to see him pitch. By this time, the Yankees, Mariners, Mets, Pirates, and Cubs had also shown interest in him. Impressed, the Dodgers eventually purchased Fernando's contract from the Mexican League team for $120,000, one-sixth of which went to Valenzuela. With the consent of his family, he began his career in the United States.

In a Strange Land

The Dodgers sent Valenzuela to their Lodi, California, farm team for his introduction to American baseball. Because Fernando did not speak English, he was lonely in the new land. He did not let it affect his pitching, however. In twenty-four innings of work, he allowed only three earned runs. That winter, the Dodgers sent him to their team in the Arizona Instructional League to help him get more experience. Campanis also sent pitcher Bobby Castillo along to teach Fernando how to throw the screwball, one of baseball's most difficult pitches. Campanis knew if Valenzuela had some kind of specialty pitch to go with his fastball and curve, it would help him immensely.

Fernando proved to be a fast learner. He became skilled at throwing the pitch in just a few months. Said Castillo, "Some guys spend years trying to learn it and this guy got it right away."[67] When he reported to the Dodgers' San Antonio club in the Class AA Texas League the next spring, Valenzuela had a new weapon at his disposal.

Fernando enjoyed his time with San Antonio. He was still extremely shy and acquired the nickname Señor Silent. However, his pitching (and hitting) quickly made him a favorite among the fans, particularly the many Mexican Americans in the city. Although he had just a 6–9 record by early July, he went 7–0 down the stretch, compiling an 0.87 earned run average and seventy-eight strikeouts in sixty-two innings. His 13–9 mark for the year was coupled with an earned run average of 3.10.

At the same time that San Antonio was getting ready for the postseason play-offs, the Dodgers, too, were making a run for the pennant. Needing pitching help for the stretch run, they called Valenzuela up from the minors to join the major-league team on September 10, 1980. Appearing in ten games in relief over the final month of the season, he performed admirably. He won two games and saved one, pitching seventeen and two-thirds innings without giving up a single run. He also struck out sixteen batters. Despite his efforts, the Dodgers came up short, losing the West title when they lost a play-off game to the Houston Astros.

An Incredible Start

Although Valenzuela impressed the Dodgers with his sparkling debut over the final month of the 1980 season, no one could have foreseen what was in store for 1981. Good things were expected of the team, but as training camp wound down, several of the club's starting pitchers were either hurt or sick. The day before the season opener, starting pitcher Jerry Reuss strained his calf muscle. With his options severely limited, manager Tommy Lasorda turned to Valenzuela. The twenty-year-old left-hander thus became the first rookie to start for Los Angeles on opening day.

Valenzuela took the mound on April 9 for his first major-league start against the defending National League West

Valenzuela signs autographs for fans in 1981, the incredible season that launched a national phenomenon known as "Fernandomania."

champion Astros. Showing a maturity far beyond his years, he breezed through the Houston lineup. When it was all over, he had thrown a five-hit, complete game shutout, defeating the Astros by a score of 2–0. As catcher Mike Scioscia ran out to the mound to congratulate his pitcher, the fans began chanting, "Fernando, Fernando." It was the beginning of a phenomenon that was to become known as "Fernandomania."

Five days later, Fernando defeated San Francisco, 7–1, for his second victory. The run scored by the Giants was the first against Valenzuela after thirty-four and one-third scoreless major-league innings. He followed up with shutouts in each of his next two starts. In the latter contest, he again defeated Houston, with his single driving home the game's only run.

With his record now standing at 4–0, Valenzuela made his next start on April 27 against the Giants. He defeated them by a 5–0 score for his third consecutive shutout. He also got three hits to help his own cause. "Is there anything he can't do?" asked Dodgers broadcaster Vin Scully.[68] Win number six came against the Montreal Expos. Fernando did not get credit for a complete game, because he was removed for a pinch hitter in the tenth inning. When the Dodgers scored five runs, he received credit for the victory, running his record to 6–0 with a 0.33 earned run average.

Valenzuela next brought his magic to New York, where he defeated the Mets, 1–0. It was his seventh straight win and fifth shutout, and his earned run average was lowered to 0.29. He was now just one win away from tying Boo Ferris's major-league record for most consecutive wins at the start of a career.

Breaking the Record

Fernando baffled hitters with his devastating screwball. He also had a unique pitching motion, which gave opposing batters reason for concern. In the middle of his delivery, with his right leg raised up in front of him, his eyes turned toward the sky as if looking for help from above. Somehow, he was able to refocus on the catcher's target in the brief fraction of a second before he released the ball.

On May 14, nearly fifty-four thousand fans jammed Dodger Stadium to see Valenzuela go after the record against the Expos. Leading 2–1 in the top half of the ninth inning with two outs and nobody on base, Fernando got careless and surrendered a game-tying home run to Andre Dawson. Luck was on his side, however. In the Dodgers' half of the inning, Pedro Guerrero led off with a homer of his own to give Los Angeles a 3–2 win and Valenzuela a share of the record.

Valenzuela's parents were in the stands at Dodger Stadium to see him attempt to set a new record on May 18. The defending world champion Philadelphia Phillies were the Dodgers' opponent that day. Fernando struggled for the first time in his brief major-league career. Future Hall of Famer Mike Schmidt homered in the first inning, and the Phillies added three more runs. Philadelphia pitcher Marty Bystrom held the Dodgers in check, and Valenzuela came out on the short end of a 4–0 score for his first big-league loss.

The law of averages began to catch up with Valenzuela after his incredible start. In a season interrupted by a two-month-long players' strike, he finished with a record of 13–7. His final win was a 3–0 whitewashing of the Atlanta Braves, giving him a

Valenzuela prepares to throw the ball using his unique pitching style—his right leg raised up in front, his eyes looking toward the sky.

rookie-record eight shutouts. His 180 strikeouts led the National League, making him the first rookie in twenty-six years to do so. He also led the league in complete games (11) and innings pitched (192) while sporting an earned run average of 2.48. To top it off, he also batted .250, an excellent average for a pitcher.

With Valenzuela leading the way, the Dodgers won the National League West title. In the postseason, he won three of four games to lead Los Angeles past Houston and Montreal and into the World Series against the Yankees. When the New Yorkers took the first two games of the Series, manager Lasorda called on Valenzuela to halt the slide in Game 3. He responded with one of his gutsiest performances, defeating the mighty Yankees, 5–4. The Dodgers came back to take the next three games and win the championship.

In recognition of his rookie heroics, Valenzuela was named the National League's Rookie of the Year. He was also voted the league's Cy Young Award winner, making him the first player to win both awards in the same year. Fernando also garnered a Silver Slugger trophy as the league's best-hitting pitcher and finished fifth in the balloting for Most Valuable Player. The Dodgers' long search for a hero for their local Mexican fans was at an end.

A Solid Career

Over the next six years, Valenzuela was one of the most successful pitchers in the National League. He won ninety-eight games, reaching a high of twenty-one in 1986 when he led the league. He started thirty-four or more games each of those seasons and struck out two hundred or more batters three times (1984, 1985, and 1986).

Although he was not as dominating as in the first half of his rookie season, Valenzuela still provided the Dodgers and their fans with many thrills. After holding out for a higher salary in 1982, he won nineteen games and compiled an earned run average of 2.87. The following February, he was eligible for salary arbitration. In this process, the player and the team each submit a figure to an impartial arbitrator. The arbitrator must select one or the other as the salary that he thinks the player deserves. No compromise is allowed, and his decision is final.

Proud of his heritage, Valenzuela dons a Mexican sombrero at a press conference after he was named the National League Rookie of the Year.

Valenzuela won his arbitration case and became the first player awarded a $1 million salary through the process. He responded by winning fifteen games, including the one that clinched the National League West title for Los Angeles.

In 1984, Valenzuela posted his first losing record at 12–17. He was not completely at fault, however, because the Dodgers supported him with few runs. His 3.03 earned run average was perhaps a better indication of how well he pitched.

The next year, Valenzuela began the season by not allowing an earned run in his first forty-one and one-third innings. In doing so, he broke a seventy-three-year-old major-league record held by former New York Giants pitcher Hooks Wiltse. The Dodgers, however, still had difficulty scoring for him. He was named Pitcher of the Month for April despite winning only two of his five decisions. He thus became the first pitcher to win the honor while posting a losing record.

In Valenzuela's twenty-one-win season of 1986, he tossed a career-high twenty complete games that also led the National

League. One of the high points of his season occurred on July 15 during the annual All-Star Game. Although the American League won the contest, 3–2, Valenzuela tied Carl Hubbell's fifty-two-year-old record by fanning five batters in a row, setting down Don Mattingly, Cal Ripken, Jesse Barfield, Lou Whitaker, and Ted Higuera.

Mediocrity

Valenzuela did not post a winning record in any of his last four seasons with Los Angeles. From 1987 through 1990, he won forty-two games while losing forty-eight. He did, however, continue to be a workhorse. From 1981 through mid-1988, he made 255 consecutive starts without missing a turn until a shoulder injury stopped the streak.

On July 29, 1990, Valenzuela had one final moment of glory with the Dodgers. Earlier that day, Oakland's Dave Stewart had tossed a no-hitter against the Toronto Blue Jays. Valenzuela took the mound against St. Louis and duplicated Stewart's feat. He defeated the Cardinals, 6–0, without allowing a single base hit. It marked the first time two separate no-hitters had been thrown on the same day since 1898.

Despite the no-hitter, Valenzuela compiled just a 13–13 mark in 1990 and a 4.59 earned run average. As a result, he was released by the Dodgers during training camp the following spring. From 1991 through 1997, he pitched with varying degrees of success with the California Angels, Baltimore Orioles, Philadelphia Phillies, San Diego Padres, and St. Louis Cardinals. After winning just two of twelve decisions in 1997, he was released by St. Louis and dropped from the major-league scene.

The Pride of Mexico

Fernando Valenzuela won 173 games in his seventeen-year major-league career. As Vin Scully said, "He wrote a lot of history during one of the Dodgers' most profitable decades in terms of victories and highlights."[69] He was one of the most popular players to don a Los Angeles uniform, and the inspiration for a whole generation of young Mexican players. As Mike Brito explained, "Before him, the Mexican players didn't have any ambitions. After they saw the success of Fernando, they all wanted to play in the big leagues. He opened the door. Young kids—north or south of the border—adore him."[70]

Although Valenzuela has not pitched in the majors since 1997, he has continued to hurl in the Mexican leagues. "Fernando is a symbol here," said Juan Aguirre, spokesman for the Hermosillo Orange Growers of Mexico's Pacific Coast League in February 2001. "He is an example on and off the field. Kids who never saw him in his best days adore him."[71]

As much as Valenzuela has given to his fans, he has received back from them in return. "The cheers keep me going," he said. "This [pitching for Hermosillo] allows me to give something to the people, whatever I have left, in return for all the support they have given me."[72]

Valenzuela hurls the ball against a Dominican Republic team as a pitcher in the Mexican leagues in 2001.

Notes

Introduction: The Transformation

1. Quoted in Bob Chieger, ed., *Voices of Baseball*. New York: New American Library, 1983, p. 35.

Chapter 1: From Bums to Royalty

2. Quoted in Geoffrey C. Ward and Ken Burns, *Baseball: An Illustrated History*. New York: Alfred A. Knopf, 1994, p. 120.
3. Quoted in Richard Whittingham, *The Los Angeles Dodgers: An Illustrated History*. New York: Harper & Row, 1982, p. 44.
4. Quoted in Whittingham, *The Los Angeles Dodgers: An Illustrated History*, p. 47.
5. Quoted in Ward and Burns, *Baseball: An Illustrated History*, p. 349.

Chapter 2: Sandy Koufax

6. Quoted in Sandy Koufax with Ed Linn, *Koufax*. New York: Viking Press, 1966, p. 38.
7. Quoted in Charles Moritz, ed., *Current Biography Yearbook: 1964*. New York: H.W. Wilson, 1964, p. 239.
8. Quoted in Moritz, *Current Biography Yearbook: 1964*, p. 239.
9. Quoted in Steve Delsohn, *True Blue*. New York: William Morrow, 2001, p. 39.
10. Quoted in Delsohn, *True Blue*, p. 43.
11. Quoted in Koufax with Linn, *Koufax*, p. 154.
12. Quoted in Delsohn, *True Blue*, p. 60.
13. Quoted in Chieger, *Voices of Baseball*, p. 169.
14. Quoted in Delsohn, *True Blue*, p. 86.

Chapter 3: Don Drysdale

15. Quoted in Chieger, *Voices of Baseball*, p. 164.
16. Quoted in Don Drysdale with Bob Verdi, *Once a Bum, Always a Dodger*. New York: St. Martin's Press, 1990, p. 18.
17. Quoted in Drysdale with Verdi, *Once a Bum, Always a Dodger*, p. 41.
18. Quoted in Drysdale with Verdi, *Once a Bum, Always a Dodger*, p. 60.
19. Quoted in Charles Moritz, ed., *Current Biography Yearbook: 1965*. New York: H.W. Wilson, 1965, p. 133.
20. Quoted in Drysdale with Verdi, *Once a Bum, Always a Dodger*, pp. 73-74.
21. Quoted in Moritz, *Current Biography Yearbook: 1965*, p. 133.
22. Quoted in Moritz, *Current Biography Yearbook: 1965*, p. 133.
23. Quoted in Moritz, *Current Biography Yearbook: 1965*, p. 134.
24. Quoted in Drysdale with Verdi, *Once a Bum, Always a Dodger*, p. 125.
25. Quoted in Delsohn, *True Blue*, p. 92.
26. Quoted in "Don Drysdale," *BaseballLibrary.com*. www.pub dim.net.
27. Quoted in "Don Drysdale," *BaseballLibrary.com*.

Chapter 4: Maury Wills

28. Quoted in Charles Moritz, ed., *Current Biography Yearbook: 1966*. New York: H.W. Wilson, 1986, p. 447.
29. Quoted in Moritz, *Current Biography Yearbook: 1966*, p. 447.
30. Quoted in Moritz, *Current Biography Yearbook: 1966*, p. 447.
31. Quoted in Tommy Holmes, *Baseball's Great Teams: The Dodgers*. New York: Collier Books, 1975, p. 173.
32. Quoted in Moritz, *Current Biography Yearbook: 1966*, p. 449.
33. Quoted in Moritz, *Current Biography Yearbook: 1966*, p. 449.
34. Quoted in David Pietrusza, Matthew Silverman, and Michael Gershman, eds., *Baseball: The Biographical Encyclopedia*, New York: Total/Sports Illustrated, 2000, p. 1,240.
35. Maury Wills and Mike Celizic, *On the Run*. New York: Carroll & Graf Publishers, 1991, p. 287.
36. Quoted in the Maury Wills Official Website. www.maury wills.com.

Chapter 5: Steve Garvey

37. Quoted in Joe Henderson, "No. 6 Steve Garvey," *Tampa Bay Online*. www.tampabayonline.net.
38. Quoted in Pietrusza, Silverman, and Gershman, *Baseball: The Biographical Encyclopedia*, p. 400.
39. Quoted in Steve Garvey with Skip Rozin, *Garvey*. New York: Times Books, 1986, p. 25.
40. Quoted in Garvey with Rozin, *Garvey*, p. 40.
41. Quoted in Garvey with Rozin, *Garvey*, p. 56.
42. Quoted in Garvey with Rozin, *Garvey*, p. 65.
43. Quoted in Garvey with Rozin, *Garvey*, p. 80.
44. Quoted in Henderson, "No. 6 Steve Garvey," *Tampa Bay Online*.
45. Quoted in Garvey with Rozin, *Garvey*, p. 201.
46. Quoted in John Kuenster, "A Crushing Defeat," *Baseball Digest*, May 2001. www.findarticles.com.

Chapter 6: Tommy Lasorda

47. Quoted in Piertrusza, Silverman, and Gershman, *Baseball: The Biographical Encyclopedia*, p. 646.
48. Quoted in Charles Moritz, ed., *Current Biography Yearbook: 1989*. New York: H.W. Wilson, 1989, p. 322.
49. Quoted in Tommy Lasorda and David Fisher, *The Artful Dodger*. New York: Arbor House, 1985, p. 3.
50. Quoted in Pietrusza, Silverman, and Gershman, *Baseball: The Biographical Encyclopedia*, p. 646.
51. Quoted in Lasorda and Fisher, *The Artful Dodger*, p. 20.
52. Quoted in Moritz, *Current Biography Yearbook: 1989*, p. 322.
53. Quoted in Hogan Chen, "Lasorda's Wild Start," *Baseball Library*. www.pubdim.net.
54. Quoted in Lasorda and Fisher, *The Artful Dodger*, p. 56.
55. Quoted in Moritz, *Current Biography Yearbook: 1989*, p. 322.
56. Quoted in Moritz, *Current Biography Yearbook: 1989*, p. 322.
57. Quoted in Delsohn, *True Blue*, p. 155.
58. Quoted in Delsohn, *True Blue*, p. 177.
59. Quoted in Delsohn, *True Blue*, p. 199.
60. Quoted in Delsohn, *True Blue*, p. 206.
61. Quoted in Delsohn, *True Blue*, p. 211.

62. Quoted in Pietrusza, Silverman, and Gershman, *Baseball: The Biographical Encyclopedia*, p. 646.
63. Quoted in Mark Miller, "Tommy Lasorda," *Salon*, October 17, 2000. www.salon.com.
64. Quoted in Miller, "Tommy Lasorda," *Salon*, October 17, 2000.

Chapter 7: Fernando Valenzuela

65. Quoted in Charles Moritz, ed., *Current Biography Yearbook: 1982*. New York: H.W. Wilson, 1982, p. 424.
66. Quoted in Eddie Rivera, "Only in America, Land of Opportunity. . ." *Inside Sports*, June 1981, p. 47.
67. Quoted in Moritz, *Current Biography Yearbook: 1982*, p. 424.
68. Quoted in Paul Click, "20 Years Ago, Fernando Valenzuela Was King of the Hill," *Baseball Digest*, July 2001, www.findarticles.com.
69. Quoted in Click, "20 Years Ago, Fernando Valenzuela Was King of the Hill," *Baseball Digest*, July 2001.
70. Quoted in Click, "20 Years Ago, Fernando Valenzuela Was King of the Hill," *Baseball Digest*, July 2001.
71. Quoted in "Fernando-mania," *CNN/Sports Illustrated*, February 4, 2001. www.sportsillustrated.cnn.com.
72. Quoted in Click, "20 Years Ago, Fernando Valenzuela Was King of the Hill," *Baseball Digest*, July 2001.

For Further Reading

Books

James Charlton, ed., *The Baseball Chronology.* New York: Macmillan, 1991. A day-by-day chronological history of baseball, from 1845 through 1990.

Ron Fimrite, *The World Series.* New York: Time, 1997. *Sports Illustrated* series volume that is a beautifully illustrated tribute to baseball's Fall Classic.

Edward Gruver, *Koufax.* Dallas, TX: Taylor Publishing Company, 2000. The biography of Sandy Koufax, the Hall of Fame left-hander, told within the framework of Game 7 of the 1965 World Series.

Roger Kahn, *The Boys of Summer.* New York: New American Library, 1973. Kahn's classic book tells the story of the great Dodger teams of the 1950s.

Harold Parrott, *The Lords of Baseball.* Marietta, GA: Longstreet Press, 2002. A unique behind-the-scenes look at major-league baseball written by the former traveling secretary and publicist of the Brooklyn Dodgers.

Ira Rosen, *Blue Skies, Green Fields: A Celebration of 50 Major League Baseball Stadiums.* New York: Clarkson Potter, 2001. This illustrated volume contains pictures and descriptions of thirty current major-league stadiums and twenty parks of the past.

Mike Shatzkin, ed., *The Ballplayers.* New York: Arbor House, 1990. The ultimate baseball biographical reference, containing more than five thousand biographies.

Works Consulted

Books

Bob Chieger, ed., *Voices of Baseball*. New York: New American Library, 1983. A collection of quotations about baseball topics ranging from baserunning to umpires.

Steve Delsohn, *True Blue*. New York: William Morrow, 2001. This volume is a collection of comments and reminiscences by members of Dodger teams of the seventies, eighties, and nineties.

Don Drysdale with Bob Verdi, *Once a Bum, Always a Dodger*. New York: St. Martin's Press, 1990. The autobiography of the Dodgers' Hall of Fame pitcher.

Steve Garvey with Skip Rozin, *Garvey*. New York: Times Books, 1986. The autobiography of baseball's "Mr. Clean."

Tommy Holmes, *Baseball's Great Teams: The Dodgers*. New York: Collier Books, 1975. This history of the Dodgers franchise covers the team from its beginnings in Brooklyn through the 1974 season.

Sandy Koufax with Ed Linn, *Koufax*. New York: Viking Press, 1966. The autobiography of one of the greatest pitchers of all time.

Tommy Lasorda and David Fisher, *The Artful Dodger*. New York: Arbor House, 1985. The inspirational story of the third-string high-school pitcher who became manager of the world champion Los Angeles Dodgers.

Charles Moritz, ed., *Current Biography Yearbook: 1964*. New York: H.W. Wilson, 1964. Library volume that contains all of the biographies published in the *Current Biography* magazine in 1964.

———Current Biography Yearbook: 1965. New York: H.W. Wilson, 1965. Library volume that contains all of the biographies published in the Current Biography magazine in 1965.

———Current Biography Yearbook: 1966. New York: H.W. Wilson, 1966. Library volume that contains all of the biographies published in the Current Biography magazine in 1966.

———Current Biography Yearbook: 1982. New York: H.W. Wilson, 1982. Library volume that contains all of the biographies published in the Current Biography magazine in 1982.

———Current Biography Yearbook: 1989. New York: H.W. Wilson, 1989. Library volume that contains all of the biographies published in the Current Biography magazine in 1989.

David Pietrusza, Matthew Silverman, and Michael Gershman, eds., Baseball: The Biographical Encyclopedia. New York: Total/Sports Illustrated, 2000. This volume contains brief biographies of more than two-thousand players, managers, umpires, and front-office figures from the national pastime's glorious history.

Geoffrey C. Ward and Ken Burns, Baseball: An Illustrated History. New York: Alfred A. Knopf, 1994. This lavishly illustrated book is the companion volume to the PBS television series of the same name.

Richard Whittingham, The Los Angeles Dodgers: An Illustrated History. New York: Harper & Row, 1982. A richly illustrated book covering the history of the Dodger franchise, with the emphasis on their first quarter-century in Los Angeles.

Maury Wills and Mike Celizic, On the Run. New York: Carroll & Graf Publishers, 1991. The revealing autobiography of the player who revolutionized the art of base stealing.

Periodicals

Eddie Rivera, "Only in America, Land of Opportunity . . ." Inside Sports, June 1981.

Internet Sources

Hogan Chen, "Lasorda's Wild Start," Baseball Library. www.pubdim.net.

Paul Click, "20 Years Ago, Fernando Valenzuela Was King of the Hill," *Baseball Digest*, July 2001. www.findarticles.com.

"Don Drysdale," *BaseballLibrary.com*. www.pubdim.net.

"Fernando-mania," *CNN/Sports Illustrated*, February 4, 2001. www.sportsillustrated.cnn.com.

Joe Henderson, "No. 6 Steve Garvey," *Tampa Bay Online*. www.tampabayonline.net.

John Kuenster, "A Crushing Defeat," *Baseball Digest*, May 2001. www.findarticles.com.

Mark Miller, "Tommy Lasorda," *Salon*, October 17, 2000. www.salon.com.

Websites

The Maury Wills Official Website (www.maurywills.com). The official home page of the former Dodgers All-Star shortstop.

Index

Picture Credits

About the Author

John F. Grabowski is a native of Brooklyn, New York. He holds a bachelor's degree in psychology from City College of New York and a master's degree in educational psychology from Teacher's College, Columbia University. He has been a teacher for thirty-one years, as well as a freelance writer specializing in the fields of sports, education, and comedy. His body of published work includes twenty-eight books; a nationally syndicated sports column; consultation on several math textbooks; articles for newspapers, magazines, and the programs of professional sports teams; and comedy material sold to Jay Leno, Joan Rivers, Yakov Smirnoff, and numerous other comics. He and his wife, Patricia, live in Staten Island with their daughter, Elizabeth.